Another Mother

From the Tales of Dan Coast

Another Mother

From the Tales of Dan Coast

By

Rodney Riesel

Published by Island Holiday Publishing
East Greenbush, NY

Special thanks to:

Pamela Guerriere

Kevin Cook

Cover Image by:

Lufimorgan at 123rf.com

Cover Design by:

Connie Fitsik

To learn about my other books friend me at

https://www.facebook.com/rodneyriesel

For Brenda,
Kayleigh, Ethan
& Peyton

Chapter One

"So you're telling me your real name is Maggie Harrison?" Dan asked the young woman on the phone. A seagull screamed in the background, and Dan turned his head toward the beach.

"Yes, that's my real name," she replied. "I'm sorry we lied to you in Haines City."

"The police officer I spoke with the other night told me your father was a lawyer in West Palm Beach. Is that true?"

"Yes."

"What's his name?"

"Harrison."

"Right. What's his first name?"

"Harrison. My father's name is Harrison Harrison."

"Well, that's just insane," said Dan. "His parents must have been pretty cruel people."

"I never knew my grandparents," said Maggie. "They died before I was born."

"Hold on a second. Maxine!" Dan Coast shouted. He sat in an Adirondack chair next to the fire pit in the backyard of his bungalow at 632 Beach View Street in Key West.

Buddy, Dan's border collie and black lab mix, lay in the hot afternoon sun on the neighbor's deck. He opened one eye when he heard his master shout but closed it soon after, knowing that it was probably nothing that involved him.

Dan picked up the tequila, Seven, and lime that was sitting on the ground to his left and took a drink. "Maxine!" he shouted again.

The back screen door swung open and Maxine stuck her head out. "What?" she shouted.

"What are you doing?" Dan asked.

"Sweeping up the dust from Colt's work. You were just in here and saw me doing it."

Colt was Colton Masters, or as he had recently come to be known, "Rick's guy." Colton was a local contractor who worked for Rick, and now Dan. He was thirty years old, had long blond hair, a dark tan, and rarely wore a shirt. Colt had been hired by Maxine to install a new front window and repair the hole in the ceiling. The window and ceiling were both damaged in a shootout between Dan and Red, and Melvin Jessup, the red-headed hit man. Dan had wanted to do the repairs himself, but because of a recent case, just didn't have the time.

"Can you get me a pen?" Dan asked.

Maxine shook her head at her fiancé's laziness. "Sure." She pulled her head back inside and let the door shut.

"Hold on one second, Maggie. My secretary is grabbing me a pen."

"I don't have much time to talk."

"It'll just be a second."

The screen door opened again and Dan looked over.

"Catch," Maxine called out. She let the pen fly.

"Really?" Dan groaned. He raised his arm as high as he could to catch the Bic ball point, but it sailed right over him. "Dammit, Maxine!"

Maxine giggled and went back inside.

"Boy, I'll tell ya, Maggie, good help is hard to find these days," Dan moaned as he climbed out of his chair and went in search of the pen. He bent over and picked it up.

"I have to go," Maggie whispered.

"What's a number where I can reach you?" Dan asked. He waited a few seconds. "Maggie … are you there?"

Dan pulled his cell away from his ear and looked at the screen. Maggie had ended the call.

"Dammit," Dan said. He sat back down in his chair and dropped his cell on top of the morning's edition of the Key West Citizen that lay on the ground to his right. He picked his glass back up and downed the remainder of his drink. "Maxine!" Dan stared at the back door in anticipation. "Maxine!"

"What!"

Dan rattled the ice in his empty glass. "Will you make me another drink?"

Maxine glared at him for a second. "Get off your dead ass and make it yourself." She let the door slam shut behind her.

"Ouch," said Dan. "Put a ring on a girl's finger and she really changes."

"I got a finger for you right here!" she shouted back, and stuck her arm out the door.

"Whoa." Dan watched as Maxine's arm disappeared back into the kitchen. He stared at his glass and drank a little of the melted ice.

Bev's back door opened.

Score, Dan thought. *Bev'll make me a drink.*

Bev stepped out onto the deck and over the dog. She stretched her arms over her head and reached for the sky. After that, she bent over and touched her toes.

Huh, thought Dan. *Pretty limber for an old lady.*

Bev wasn't really that old; she was just a few weeks away from turning sixty. Dan and Maxine had discussed throwing her a surprise birthday party for the special day, but were having a hard time deciding if she would love it, or hate it.

"Good afternoon, neighbor!" Dan called out.

Bev looked over and waved.

"Care for a drink?" Dan asked.

Bev looked at her wristwatch. "Sure," she said. "Why not?"

"Will ya make me one too?" Dan rattled the ice in his glass as he spoke.

Bev shook her head. "I figured as much." She walked across the deck and down the steps, with Buddy right behind her.

Dan glared at his dog. "Man's best friend," he grumbled.

When Bev reached her lazy beach bum of a neighbor, she held out her hand for his glass.

Dan flashed his pearly whites and handed her the empty glass. "Thank you," he said.

"Yeah," Bev replied. She looked down at Buddy, who was standing next to her. "Lay down, Buddy."

Buddy did as he was commanded.

"Good boy," said Bev.

"Yeah, good boy," Dan mocked.

Bev turned and made her way up the gravel path to the kitchen door.

"Why is it you listen to everyone but me?" Dan asked his dog.

Buddy stretched his neck and rubbed the side of his head against Dan's shin.

Dan leaned forward in his chair and patted the dog on the head. He let out a sigh. "You are a good boy," he said.

Buddy rested his head on Dan's foot, and closed his eyes.

Dan picked the newspaper back up and read through the headlines. He finally made it to the most important part of the morning paper, the comics. He read down through the entire page before noticing that Bev had never returned with his drink. He folded the paper and dropped it back on the ground. "What the Christ?" he groaned, as he pulled himself up out of the old Adirondack chair. "What the hell is she doing in there?"

Dan walked up the pathway and pulled open the screen door. Maxine and Bev were standing in the living room, staring out through the window, at a shirtless Colton

Masters. Their arms were folded in front of them and their head were slightly cocked. It was as though the two women were admiring a piece of beautiful artwork. Dan stepped quietly into the kitchen and let the door ease shut behind him.

Colton turned and bent over to pick up his two-foot level. Bev jabbed Maxine in the ribs with her elbow. Like a well-choreographed synchronized swim team, the ladies' heads slowly cocked in the other direction. Dan thought about how this scenario would play out if it were him and Red staring out the window at a shirtless woman.

Dan tip-toed closer. "What's going on?" he asked.

"I'm not doing anything!" Maxine shouted, as she spun around, startled, on her heels.

Bev also turned around. "I was just making you that drink," she said, and went toward the bar.

Dan stretched his neck to see out the window. "Watchoo girls lookin' at?" he asked. "Something out there I should see?"

Maxine's face was beet red. "We, uh … we, uh—"

"We, uh. We, uh," Dan aped.

"You two disgust me, treating that poor guy like he's just some piece of meat."

"Hey, I'm single," Bev said, throwing Maxine under the bus. "I don't know what her problem is."

"Wow, really?" said Maxine. "That's how it is?"

Bev handed Dan his fresh drink.

"Thanks, Bev," Dan said. He took a sip of the drink as he glared at Maxine. "Maybe if you weren't in here gawking at the help, *you* could have found time to prepare my drink."

"I wasn't gawking," Maxine argued. "And shut up anyway."

Dan laughed and walked over to give Maxine a kiss. "I'm just ribbing you. Calm down."

Maxine turned her head when Dan came in for the kiss. "I don't like to be ribbed."

"Sorry," Dan said, and kissed her on the cheek. "They claim it's for your pleasure."

"You're a pig."

"Never said I wasn't." Dan took another sip of his drink. "Are you gonna make yourself a drink, Bev?"

Bev didn't answer.

Dan turned around. "Are you gonna—"

Bev was once again focused on the young man outside.

Dan snapped his fingers. "Hey, dirty old lady, are you gonna make yourself a drink?"

"Yeah, I better," said Bev. "If I stare out that window any longer I'm going to need a cigarette."

Maxine giggled.

"On that note," Dan said, "I'm going back outside."

Dan was almost back to his chair when he heard his cell phone ring. He ran to the phone and picked it up. He looked at the screen; it was an unknown number again. "Hello?"

"Mr. Coast, I only have a second," Maggie explained.

"But—"

"Meet me in West Palm Beach at E.R. Bradley's Saloon on Thursday at noon."

"But—" The call ended. "Dammit!"

"What's the matter?" Maxine asked. She and Bev were just walking out the back door. They each had a drink in their hand.

Dan slid his phone back into his pocket. "I have to drive up to West Palm Thursday morning."

"Are you kidding?" Maxine asked.

"Nope."

"You just got back."

"I know, but this might be important."

"Might be?"

Maxine took a seat in the other Adirondack chair, and Dan got up so Bev could have his chair. He got a folding lawn chair out of the shed and sat down.

"Let me start from the beginning," said Dan. "On our way to Bonifay last week we stopped in a little hotel in Haines City."

"I remember," said Maxine.

"We met this young girl and guy. They said they were on the run from her father. The girl—Maggie Harrison—had some bruises on her face. They claimed her father had given them to her."

"That's horrible," Bev said.

"Long story short," Dan continued, "early the next morning the cops showed up at the hotel. They arrested the boyfriend, and took the girl home to her father."

"Is the girl a minor?" Maxine asked.

"No," Dan answered.

"Then what did they arrest him for?"

"One of the cops told us that the kid had killed the girl's mother, and that he had kidnapped Maggie."

"Did you get the impression he had kidnapped her?" Bev asked.

"No," Dan replied, shaking his head. "They seemed like they were telling the truth."

"And that was the girl on the phone," Maxine surmised.

"Yes. She claims that it was her father that killed her mother, and that he set up her boyfriend. Now she thinks her father is trying to kill *her*."

"Oh my goodness," said Bev.

"So, you see why I have to go?"

"I guess," said Maxine. "But when you get back home, you better be home for a while."

"I promise." Dan sat sipping his drink and thinking. "You think Colton will be done here by Thursday?"

"I don't know," Maxine responded. "Why do you ask?"

"No reason," said Dan. "Just wondering."

Bev snorted.

"Shut up, Bev," said Dan.

Chapter Two

Dan steered his black 2012 Porsche 911 S Cabriolet into the crushed-stone parking lot of Red's Bar and Grill, and backed into a spot across from the front door. He climbed out of the convertible and made his way across the parking lot. He walked up the steps and pushed open the door. He removed his Ray-Ban Wayfarers and hung them over the front of his black T-shirt.

There was a couple in their sixties at a four-top to his left, and a twenty-something couple were seated at a table near them. Everyone had drinks and food, and seemed to be enjoying themselves. "Legalize It" by Peter Tosh was playing on the old Wurlitzer.

There was also a gentleman seated by himself at the bar. He wore camouflage cargo shorts and a chocolate-brown T-shirt. The guy was about Dan's age, with black hair cut short, similar to Dan's, with a lot of gray at the temples. He appeared to Dan to be part Asian. The guy was three seats down from Dan's favorite stool. This made Dan very happy. There's nothing worse than walking into your favorite bar and seeing some other guy sitting on your favorite stool.

The older gentleman at the four-top glanced up as Dan walked by, and nodded. Dan nodded back.

Dan climbed aboard his stool and rested his forearms on the bar. He looked down at the other barfly's drink. It was empty.

The guy noticed Dan looking and said, "The bartender went into the kitchen a while ago and hasn't been back."

Dan jumped off his stool and walked around behind the bar. He made himself a drink, and then made one for the other guy. The guy reached into his pocket for money.

Dan put up his hand. "This one's on the house."

"Thanks, pal," the guy said.

Dan looked around the dining room. "Anybody else need a drink?"

The two guys raised their hands.

"What do ya got there?" Dan asked the older gentleman.

"My wife and I both have LandSharks," he replied.

"Margarita on the rocks here," the twenty-something called out.

Dan made the margarita and grabbed two LandSharks out of the cooler and headed to the tables. "Here ya go, folks," he said, placing a drink in front of each of them. "On the house."

They all thanked him, and Dan returned to his stool.

The kitchen door opened. "Hey, pal," Red said. "When did you get here?"

"Just walked in the door," Dan replied.

"I see you made yourself a drink."

"Yut."

Red looked at the other guy. "You ready?"

"I made *him* one too," said Dan. "And I got the tables each a drink."

"Hey, thanks," Red said. "Did you put the money in the register?"

"I told everyone the drinks were on the house."

"You're a dick."

"My mother's dyi—"

"Shut up."

Dan snickered and took a sip of his drink. "Can you have Jocko make me a fish sandwich and fries?"

"Sure." Red side-stepped to his right and took a few steps back. He pushed open the kitchen door. "Jocko! Order up! Fish sandwich and fries."

"Yeah!" Jocko hollered back.

Red let the swinging door swing shut, and returned to the bar. He grabbed a mug off the back bar and poured himself a cup of coffee. "You been over to the hospital to see Skip?"

"Not yet," said Dan. "I was gonna stop over later today."

"I'll go with you. Should we bring him anything?"

"Like what?"

"I don't know."

"Dirty magazines," said the guy down the bar.

Dan looked over. "What?"

"Dirty magazines," he repeated. "That's what I brought one of my friends once when he was in the hospital."

"I'll keep that in mind. Thanks," said Dan.

"Don't mention it." The guy went back to is drink.

"The reason I stopped in—"

"Crap," Red interrupted.

"Crap, what?"

"I was just hoping you stopped in for no reason."

"What's that supposed to mean?"

"Whenever there's a reason, it's never anything good. What is it this time?"

"We gotta run up to West Palm Thursday morning."

"We just got back," said Red with much frustration. "And I told you, I got a date Friday night."

"We'll be back Thursday night … I promise."

"Oh, well, if you *promise*," Red responded sarcastically. "You know that means nothing to me when you say that. You are in no way what I would consider a man of his word."

"Ouch," said Dan. "That hurts. I'll pick you up at six on Thursday morning."

"I'm not going," Red argued.

"I'll go," said the stranger.

"Thanks, pal," said Dan, "but he's going."

"I'm not going," Red argued.

"We'll get breakfast on the way," Dan coaxed.

"No."

"I'll pencil you in."

"Don't pencil me nothing," said Red.

"You can pencil me in, if you want," said the stranger.

Dan put up his hand. "Thanks again, but no."

The guy shrugged. "Suit yourself." The guy downed the rest of his drink and slid off the back of his stool. "Thanks for the drink, pal." He turned and Dan and Red watched him until he was out the door.

"You ever see him before?" Dan asked.

Red shook his head.

Dan got off his stool and hurried to the door. He opened it a crack and peeked out. He watched the stranger walk to his car—a black Volkswagen Passat with Texas plates—get in, and drive out of the parking lot.

"Weird," Dan said, returning to his seat.

"Ah, you think everybody's weird," said Red.

"Everybody *is* weird. That guy just seemed a little weirder than most."

"He was just trying to be friendly."

"He offered to ride to West Palm with me. That's nuts. He's probably a serial killer."

"You should have taken him up on the offer, because now you're going to West Palm alone."

"No … you're coming with me." Dan looked up at the clock on the wall over the back bar, between the glass racks. "Let's head over to the hospital and get that out of the way."

"Get it out of the way?" Red asked with surprise. "Do you even hear yourself when you speak?"

21

"What?"

"You don't refer to seeing a sick friend in the hospital as *getting it out of the way*."

"Maybe *you* don't."

Jocko walked through the kitchen door with Dan's fish sandwich and fries. "Here ya go, Coast," he said, sliding the plate across the bar.

"Silverware?" Dan asked.

"What about it?" Jocko asked, and went back into the kitchen.

"Boy, he's a real people person," said Dan.

Red grabbed a fork and knife from under the bar and tossed it in front of Dan. "Yeah," he agreed. "I think you both went to the same school of manners."

"Is there a school of manners?"

"Probably." Red looked over his shoulder at the clock. "Cindy should be here in the next few minutes, then we can leave."

Dan took a bite of his sandwich. "Good."

"Should we stop and get Skip some dirty magazines?" Red asked.

"No, that would be stupid."

"I don't know, that guy seemed to think—"

"You mean the serial killer? Yeah let's take his advice."

"Well, if I'm ever in the hospital, you can bring me dirty magazines."

"I probably won't. I probably won't even come and see you."

"Wow! And you want me to ride up to West Palm Beach with you."

"Does that mean you're going?"

"I guess."

"Then I'll bring you dirty magazines when you're in the hospital."

"Thanks."

Chapter Three

Cindy Leonard arrived at work a few minutes after Dan finished his lunch. A few minutes after that, Dan and Red jumped in Dan's car and headed for the hospital.

"We should really bring Skip something," Red said.

"I'm not stopping to buy dirty magazines," Dan shot back.

"Maybe we should bring him a cheeseburger from Wendy's," Red offered. "He loves cheeseburgers."

"I guess that would be fine—wait, are we stopping for him, or for you?"

"Well, I mean … I could eat."

"You just sat on the other side of the bar watching me eat my lunch. Why didn't you get yourself something?"

"I wasn't in the mood for that crap."

"That crap? Wow! It's your bar."

"Yeah, exactly. And I get sick of eating there."

Dan took a left onto United Street. He adjusted his rearview mirror and stared at the car behind him.

Red noticed Dan's eyes darting from the mirror to the street, and back. He turned around and looked behind them. "What are you looking at back there?"

"Remember that weirdo at the bar?"

"You mean other than you?"

"Yeah, dickhead, other than me."

"The friendly guy? What about him?"

"I think he's following us."

Red looked over his shoulder again.

"Stop looking," Dan scolded.

"Why?" Red asked. He waved to the guy behind them. The guy waved back.

"What the Christ are you doing?" Dan asked.

"I just waved to him," Red replied. "I think it *is* him."

Red started to wave again, but Dan slapped his hand down.

"Knock it off!" he warned.

"Ow!" Red shouted, rubbing the back of his hand. "What did you do that for?"

"The guy is following us, and you're waving at him," said Dan. "Who does that?"

"Friendly people," Red answered. "Like me … and that guy back there."

"I'm gonna try and lose him."

"Shouldn't we find out what he wants?"

"I don't care what he wants."

Dan flipped on his blinker to turn left at Duvall Street, but then yanked the wheel right. He floored it and slid around the corner. He took a quick right onto Catherine Street and then a left onto Simonton Street. Dan slammed on the brakes and pulled a hard left into a parking lot. He drove around behind the Florida Department of Health and exited the parking lot onto Virginia Street.

"Any sign of him?" Dan asked.

Red continued to stare out over the back of the Porsche. "Nope. I think ya lost him."

"Learned that little move from Jason Bourne," Dan said proudly.

"You mean the 'driving through a parking lot' move?" Red asked. "Real tricky."

"Lost him, didn't I?"

"Yeah, and it's a good thing too. We sure wouldn't have wanted him to know we were going to Wendy's."

"Are you saying we never had trouble at Wendy's before?" Dan asked, recalling the time two hit men tried to take them out at Wendy's.

"Once in a lifetime event," Red said. "Hey, and didn't you propose to me there?"

"I believe I did."

"So that makes two weddings you haven't set a date for."

Dan pulled into the Wendy's parking lot and into a spot near the building. He shut off the engine and Red climbed out of the car.

"You coming in?" Red asked.

"No. I just ate."

"You could still come in with me."

"Just go," Dan groaned.

"Fine," said Red, turning and heading inside.

It wasn't two minutes later when Dan saw the black Passat enter the Wendy's parking lot. "Son of a bitch," he whispered to himself. He watched as the Passat drove slowly in front of him, turned, drove behind him, and parked in the spot next to him.

The guy in the Passat lowered his passenger side window and looked across the seat at Dan. "Hey, I thought I lost you guys for a second," said the Asian guy with a smile.

"Ya don't say," Dan replied.

"Yeah. You went into that parking lot and I almost lost ya."

"Weird."

He put his car in park and shut off the engine. "What are you guys doing, getting lunch?"

Dan nodded his head.

"I like the Baconator," said the guy.

"No kiddin'?"

"Yeah." The guy nervously looked around the parking lot.

"Is there something I can help you with, pal?" Dan asked.

"What do you mean?"

"What do you mean, what do I mean? You're following us around like some kind of nut case. Back at Red's you offered to drive to West Palm Beach with me. I don't even know you."

"I'm Richard Bong."

"Yeah, I don't fuckin' care," said Dan. "I think you've been *hittin'* the bong a little too much."

Richard chuckled. "I've heard all the bong jokes."

"I bet you have. Now, why don't you just start up your car and move on before I get really pissed."

"You're Dan Coast, right?"

Dan opened his door and started getting out of the car. "That's it," he said, "and I've had just about enough of you." As Dan walked around the back of Richard's car, he noticed Red exiting Wendy's. His hands were full of takeout bags and a drink carrier.

Dan yanked open Richard's door. "Get out, asshole," he said.

"I don't want any trouble," Richard said, putting up his hands in surrender.

"Too late," Dan said. He grabbed Richard by the shirt and pulled him out of the car.

Richard kept his hands up. "Really, I don't want any trouble."

"What's going on?" Red asked.

"This asshole was still following us."

"Ouch," said Richard.

Red tried to get between Dan and Richard. He managed to save his own drink, but his Frosty and Skip's soda toppled off the drink carrier and splattered on the blacktop. "Dammit!" Red hollered. "Now look what you've done." Red shoved Dan backwards with his right forearm, and pinned Richard to his car with his left. Richard was still in a surrendering stance.

"Is Gene Coast your father?" Richard asked.

Dan cocked his head. "Yeah. Why?"

"He's my father too," said Richard.

Red relaxed his forearm.

"What?" Dan asked.

"I think you're my brother," Richard said.

"But, you're Chinese," said Dan.

"I'm Vietnamese," Richard corrected.

Red looked at Dan. "Your mom ever been to Vietnam?" he asked.

"No, ya moron," Dan shot back, "but my dad has."

"Ooooh," Red said, when the light bulb came on.

"How old are you?" Dan asked.

"Forty-six."

Dan counted the years back in his head. "That's when he was there, all right."

"How long have he and your mom been married?" Red asked.

"Forty-four years," Dan replied.

"Well, that's good."

"Yeah, that's just great."

Red sat his food bags on Richard's hood and then flattened out the wrinkles he and Dan had put in the man's shirt. "Sorry about that."

"Don't worry about it," Richard responded. He pushed himself away from the car.

"So, what makes you think that we have the same father?" Dan asked.

"My mother, Tran, died last year, from cancer," Richard explained. "Before she died she told me that an American soldier by the name of Gene Coast was my real father. After she died, I started looking for him. It wasn't hard. All it took was a couple Google searches. I found out I had two half-brothers, and four half-sisters. I know our other brother died when he was little, so I decided to contact you first, instead of our father."

Dan sighed loudly and looked up at the clear blue sky. He dropped his head and rubbed his temples. This was a lot of unexpected information to take in. He heard the crumpling paper and looked back up to see Red trying to reach quietly into one of the food bags.

"Sorry," Red whispered. "I'm hungry. You guys pretend I'm not here."

Dan shook his head. "You don't have an accent," he pointed out. "How long have you been in America?"

"My mother and the man I thought was my real father, Kim Bong, escaped North Vietnam when I was two years old. We came to the United States … Texas."

"Is your father still alive, this Kim Bong?"

"No, he died ten years ago."

"I don't know what to think about all this," said Dan. "I need to talk to my dad."

"Of course," said Richard. "My mother's maiden name was Pham. Our father would remember her by that name."

"How long are you in town? And stop saying '*our* father.'"

"Sorry. I'll be here until Sunday morning."

"Where are you staying?"

"At The Atlantic Inn … at the end of—"

"I know where it is."

"Shouldn't he stay with you?" Red asked.

Dan shot Red a look.

"He's your brother, after all," Red said.

"No," said Richard. "The hotel is fine. I wouldn't want to impose."

"I don't know that he's really my brother," Dan argued. "He just shows up and—"

"Nonsense," Red cut in. "You can stay with me until Dan makes sure you're his brother."

"No," said Dan.

"You don't have to do that," said Richard.

"It's no trouble at all," said Red.

"What the Christ!" said Dan. "I can't believe this is happening."

"I know," said Red. "Isn't it great?" Red jammed the remainder of his double cheeseburger into his mouth. He sipped his soda through the straw.

Dan was at a loss for words. That was a new feeling for him.

"So then, you're going to give our dad a call?" Richard asked.

"Yeah, but I toldja to stop calling him *our* dad. For now he's just my dad."

"You got it," Richard agreed.

"Why don't you go back to your hotel," Red suggested, "and Dan and I will pick you up around five this afternoon. We're on our way to visit a friend in the hospital right now."

"Sounds like a plan," said Richard. "I'll meet you at The Atlantic Inn at five."

Dan turned without saying anything more to Richard and walked back around to his car and got in. Red picked up the bags of food and joined Dan in the car. Dan started the car and drove out of the driveway.

"Isn't this awesome?" asked Red, his mouth full of his second burger.

"What?" Dan asked. His mind was a million miles away.

"I said, isn't this awesome."

"Isn't what awesome?"

"You have a brand new brother."

"He's not my brother."

"How do you know?"

"My dad would have said something."

"Maybe your dad didn't know."

"He doesn't even look like me."

"He kinda does."

"He's Vietnamese!"

"Yeah, he's like the Vietnamese version of you," Red argued. "Did you hear him when you called him an asshole? He said, 'Ouch.'"

"Yeah, so?"

"That's what *you* say. You say 'ouch' all the time."

"A lot of people say 'ouch.' He also said 'sounds like a plan.' You think he might be Skip's brother as well?"

"Oh my God! I didn't even think of that. What if him and Skip are both your brothers?"

"Holy shit, you're stupid."

Dan pulled into the parking lot of the Lower Keys Medical Center and into the first parking spot he found.

The two men walked across the parking lot and into the building. They rode the elevator up to the third floor.

"Skip Stoner's room?" Dan asked the nurse at the nurse's station.

She pointed at the room directly across from her. "Right there," she said, and went back to her computer monitor.

Dan and Red walked cautiously into Skip's room. Skip lay in the hospital bed with his fingers laced behind his head. His eyes shot their way as they entered.

"Yo, dudes!" said Skip. "What's up?"

"How ya doin', pal," Red asked.

"Still breathin'," Skip answered. "All my parts are still here." He showed his hands and arms and patted his legs. He grabbed his crotch. "Yup, everything's still attached."

Red stepped closer and placed the Wendy's bag on a bedside tray with wheels. "Brought ya some grub," he said, as he did his best to maneuver the bulky stand closer to Skip.

"Thanks, Red Man!"

"When they letting you out of here?" Dan asked.

"Couple days, I guess. They want to run a few more tests. The docs say I got a touch of the ole traumatic brain injury. They're just trying to determine how bad."

"It's not like anyone will notice," Dan joked.

"Ha! You got that right, Red Man."

"Dan," Dan said, correcting his friend.

"What?" Skip asked.

"You called me Red Man," Dan responded.

Skip laughed again. "Huh. I guess that's the brain injury talking. They said I might be a little confused for a while." Skip unrolled the top of the Wendy's bag and reached inside. He pulled out a double cheeseburger. "Just what the doctor ordered. Hey, there's no Coke!"

"There was one. But—" Red caught Dan's disapproving glance. "Never mind. I'll get you one out of the vending machine." Red exited the room and returned shortly with a canned Coke. He popped the top and set it on the tray.

"Thanks, dude," said Skip. "You're more helpful than some of the nurses around here. And better looking too."

"Christ, you do have traumatic brain injury," Dan observed.

Red fiddled with the two IV lines leading to the back of Skip's hand. "What do they got you on?" he asked.

"One's something for the pain. I don't remember what the other one was for."

"What pain?" Dan asked.

"Had some pretty bad headaches since the injury," Skip replied. "Oh! That reminds me, how's Mrs. Stewart doing?"

"She's good," Dan replied. "She's supposed to be back in Key West tomorrow, and then she's going to stay in Georgia with one of her kids for a while."

"That's good," said Skip. "How's Mr. Stewart?"

Red and Dan looked at each other for a second, and then back at Skip.

"He's dead," Dan said.

"Oh, man. That's too bad. How did it happen? I don't remember much."

Red said, "You—"

"He broke his neck," Dan interjected.

Skip shook his head slowly. "Damn, that's terrible."

"Yeah," Red agreed. "Terrible."

Skip bit into the burger and chewed as he spoke. "So, what have you guys been up to?" he asked.

"On Thursday we're running—" said Red.

"Nothing," Dan cut in.

Red gave him a dirty look.

"Not doing much of anything," Dan reiterated.

"Yeah, we're not doin' nothin'," said Red. "Although! Dan may have a new brother. His name is Richard Bong."

Dan clenched his teeth angrily. "You and your friggin' mouth," he muttered.

"A new brother?" Skip questioned. "Isn't your mom a little old for that?"

"He's not my mother's child," Dan clarified. "He's just my father's ... if the guy's even telling the truth."

"He's Vietnamese," Red said.

"Vietnamese twins? So there's two of them?" Skip asked. "They're attached? I'm confused."

"That's Siamese twins," Dan said. "This guy is *Vietnamese*."

"Oh ... okay," Skip said, shaking his head. "And how is that possible?"

"My dad was stationed in Vietnam before him and my mother met. This guy's mother told him that my father was also his father."

"Crazy, dude," said Skip. "Richard Bong." He chuckled. "Bong."

"Speaking of fathers," Red asked, "where's your father, Skip?"

"He was here yesterday, and this morning," Skip said. "He had to get back to Jacksonville."

"I was hoping to meet him," said Red.

"Yeah, me too," said Dan.

"And I would like to meet your new brother," Skip said.

"Let me just find out if he really is my brother before I go introducing him to everyone."

"Why would he lie about it?" Red asked.

"Think about it, Red," Dan responded. "When somebody wins the lottery, like I did, it brings out the kooks and the scam artists. I should know: they poured out of the woodwork, until I took steps to safeguard my privacy. Money is the best reason to lie."

"How would he know you won the lottery?"

Skip just looked on as the two men bickered.

"He said he Googled my family," Dan reminded Red.

"But you always told me that you didn't have your name released to the media when you won," Red argued.

"You can only remain totally anonymous in a handful of states. And New York isn't one of them. I'm sure my name is still on the lottery database."

"I guess. But he seemed like a really nice guy."

"You think everyone is a nice guy."

"Most people are."

"No, they're not."

"He offered to ride up to West Palm Beach with you on Thur—"

"Who's going to West Palm Beach?" Skip shouted.

"Um," Red said.

Dan glared at his big-mouthed friend.

"You might as well tell him now," Dan said.

"Dan and I are running up to West Palm on Thursday," Red explained.

"Why?" Skip asked.

Red looked at Dan. "Because that girl from the hotel in Haines City called him."

"That Maggie chick?"

"That's the one," said Dan.

"What did she want?"

"She thinks her father is trying to kill her," Red said.

"And her boyfriend killed her mother?" Skip asked.

"No," Dan replied. "She says it was her father who killed her mother and he framed her boyfriend for it."

Skip scratched his head. "Yeah … confusing, dude." He pulled back his covers and swung his legs over the edge of the bed.

"Whoa, whoa!" Dan said. "Where the hell do you think you're going?"

"With you guys, to West Palm Beach."

"I don't think so, pal," Dan responded. He grabbed Skip's ankles and tossed them back onto the bed. "Get your ass right back in bed."

"Really, dude?" Skip asked.

"Really, dude," Dan answered. "We can do this on our own."

"Or maybe with a little help from Dan's new brother," said Red.

"He's not going with us!"

Skip picked the half-eaten burger up off his tray and took a bite. The expression on his face as he chewed was one of total sadness.

"Sorry, Skip," Dan said. "You can go next time."

"I can't believe I'm being replaced," said Skip morosely.

"You're not being replaced," Dan assured him. "Richard isn't even going with us."

"I hope not, dude. That would really hurt."

Dan pulled the covers back up over Skip's legs. "You have nothing to worry about, Skip." He patted his friend's leg. "We gotta take off."

"Enjoy those burgers," Red added. "We'll stop back and check on you when we get back from West Palm."

Skip nodded his head sadly.

Dan and Red turned and walked away. When they were almost to the door, Red stopped and smacked himself in the forehead with the palm of his hand.

"Ha!" Red shouted. "I just got it."

"Just got what?" Dan asked.

"A Stoner is worried about being replaced by a Bong," Red answered, as he continued to chuckle. "You can't make this shit up."

"Not funny, dude!" Skip shouted.

Chapter Four

Dan pulled into his driveway fifteen minutes after dropping Red back off at his bar. Colton Masters' tools had been picked up, and he was gone for the day.

Maxine!" Dan shouted, as he walked through the front door. "Maxine!"

"What!" Maxine hollered back from the bathroom.

"Where are you?" Dan headed for the bar to make himself a drink.

"In the bathroom!"

"What are ya doin'?"

"I'll be right out."

Dan carried his glass to the fridge to grab some ice. On his way back to the dining room he heard the toilet flush. He poured himself a shot of tequila and topped it off with 7UP.

"Why do you do that?" Maxine asked, as she entered the room.

"Do what?"

"Holler my name every time you walk through the damn door."

"So I know where you are, I guess." Dan sipped his drink and then held up the glass. "You want one?"

"No," Maxine replied. "And why can't you just look around the house for me before you start yelling? It's a small house. There's only five rooms."

"That seems like an awful lot of work, when I could just stand there and shout your name."

Maxine shook her head. "For you, I guess it would be a lot of work."

"What's that mean?"

"Nothing."

"You sure you don't want a drink? You seem like something is bothering you."

"Yeah, and it started the minute someone started shouting my name."

"Ouch—oh yeah, that reminds me—I have to call my dad."

"*Have* to? Why?"

"Some guy showed up at Red's today and claims to be my half-brother."

Maxine raised an eyebrow. "Really?" Her expression said *why would anyone claim to be related to you?*

"Why are you making that face?" Dan asked.

Maxine quickly wiped the look away. "What face?"

"Never mind. Anyway … he's Asian."

"Asian?"

"Vietnamese."

"Vietnamese?"

"Yes."

"And he says he's your brother?"

"Half-brother."

"And your dad served in Viet—"

"Yes."

"Huh."

"Yeah."

"You're going to call your dad and ask if this guy could be telling the truth?"

"That's the plan."

"Is this going to cause a problem between your mother and father?"

"My mother and father weren't married until after my father returned to the states, so, I hope not."

"How old is he?"

"Forty-six."

"What's his name?"

"Richard Bong." Dan paused, then added: "Please feel free to make the obligatory drug joke."

Maxine ignored him. "You want me to leave the room while you make the call?"

"No. Why would I want you to do that?"

"I thought you might want some privacy."

"I may need you as back-up." Dan reached into the side pocket of his cargo shorts and removed his cell phone. He sat down in his recliner and placed his drink on the end table beside him. He took a deep breath and exhaled. "Here goes nothing." He dialed his father's cell.

"Hello?" said his father.

"Hey, Dad. What's goi—"

"Ha! Gotcha! Please leave your name, number, and a brief message and I'll get back to you." *Beep*.

"Good one, Dad," said Dan dryly. "Hey, I got a couple questions for ya. Can you give me a call when you get this message? It's Dan. Bye." Dan hung up and dialed his mother's cell. Her voice mail picked up as well.

"Hello. You have reached Peg Coast. Please lea— what? I'm setting up my voice mail! This is Peg Coa—no! Quit hollering my name every time you come in the damn house! Give me a second. This is Peg Coast. Please le—" *Beep*.

"Hey, Mom. It's Dan. Give me a call." Dan hung up once again and dialed his parents land line.

"Hello?" Peg answered.

"Hey, Mom."

"Hi, Danny. Did you just call my cell phone?"

"Yes, Mom. Why didn't you answer it?"

"I thought it might be one of those scammers, like they talked about on the '60 Minutes.'"

"Didn't the caller ID say it was me?"

"Yes, but Steve Kroft said they can make it look like it's someone you know, so I haven't been answering it."

"I wouldn't worry about it, Mom," Dan assured her. "Is Dad around?"

"He went fishing with Mort and Victor."

"Does he have his cell phone with him?"

"Yes, but he probably has it off."

"Why would he have it off?"

"So the battery doesn't run down."

"When is he supposed to be back?"

"Tomorrow night."

"Can you have him give me a call when he gets in?"

"I guess," Peg sighed.

"Why did you say it like that?"

"Oh nothing."

"Mom, what's the matter?"

"Everyone just calls to talk to your father. No one calls to talk to me."

"Everyone, like who?"

"Your sisters. They only stop over if your father's home."

"When is he *not* home?"

"When he goes fishing."

"When was the last time he went fishing, Mom?"

"Oh, I don't know. I guess it's been awhile."

"Then how do you know that no one stops over if he's not home? He's always home."

"Well when you say it like that …"

"Is there something you want to talk about, Mom?" Dan asked.

"No, I guess not," she sighed once again.

Dan glanced over at Maxine. "Oh, Mom, Maxine wanted to talk to you about something." He tossed Maxine his cell phone. "There ya go, babe. Thanks for backing me up." He grabbed his drink and hurried out the back door before she could object.

Dan turned his Adirondack chair around so he could stare out past his yard, and over the beach at the ocean. He stretched his legs out in front of him and crossed them at the ankles. He watched as the tourists walked up and down the beach. After about twenty minutes his drink was empty and he wanted another. He thought about shouting Maxine's name, but had already been warned about that. Dan wondered if his mother and Maxine had ended their call—and if he'd catch hell for putting her on the spot.

Dan sat and people-watched as the ice in his glass slowly melted. When there was enough water, he took a small sip. He looked back over his shoulder at the kitchen door. He wished he had his cell phone so he could call Bev. Maybe she would make him a drink. He wondered where Julian Thompson was. School was out. The young neighbor boy had made Dan drinks before. He'd been there the day before to pick up the dog shit, per an agreement they'd made, but wouldn't be back until Thursday.

Dan climbed out of his chair with a groan and went toward the house. When he got to the screen, he stealthily looked inside. He saw no sign of Maxine, so he carefully opened the door and went inside. He tiptoed across the kitchen floor as quietly as he could. He knew if Maxine was still on the phone, he might have to speak to his mother once again. Dan peeked around the corner into the dining room; the coast was clear. He hurried to the bar and made himself another drink.

"What are you doing?" Maxine asked.

Dan spun around. "Making myself a drink."

"I didn't hear you come in." Maxine stood at the entrance to the hallway. "How many drinks does that make today?"

"I don't know. Why?"

"How many?"

"Five."

"Put the glass down."

Dan chuckled. "Good one."

"Put. The. Glass. Down."

"Are you serious?"

"Do I look serious?"

"Kinda."

"Then put the glass down. You're done for the day."

"Ouch. Have a nice conversation with my mom?"

"As a matter of fact, I did. She's a little ditzy, but I like her and I think she likes me. She's actually a pretty cool mom."

"I know. After all, she gave birth to me."

"I don't hold that against her. She asked if you were still going to meetings."

"What did you tell her?"

"I told her you hadn't been in a few weeks."

"Why the Christ did you tell her that?" Dan sat his empty glass back down on the bar.

"Because she asked."

"You could have lied. That's what I do."

Maxine cocked her head. "Really?"

"I mean … uh, not to you."

"Yeah, right."

"Just to my mom."

"And to yourself."

Dan heard his cell phone ring. The ring tone was coming from Maxine's front pocket. Maxine reached in and pulled out the cell. She looked at the caller ID.

"It's Red," Maxine informed Dan.

Dan held out his hand, but Maxine answered the phone instead. She put it on speaker. "Hello?"

"Maxine?" Red asked.

"Yes."

"It's Red."

"I know."

"Is Dan there?"

"Yes."

"Um, can I talk to him?"

"He's busy right now. Can I give him a message?"

Dan glared at his fiancée.

"I was just wonder if he wanted to come over to the bar tonight and keep me company."

"I'm sorry, Red. Dan won't be able to make it. He's already had five drinks today, and he's going to an AA meeting in the morning."

Dan relaxed his shoulders in defeat and sighed.

"Oh … okay," said Red. "Just tell him I called."

"I sure will." Maxine hung up the cell and tossed it to Dan. "There's a meeting tomorrow morning at the Big Pine Methodist Church at eight o'clock."

"That's the place I go for my Monday meetings," said Dan.

"And now it's where you go for your Wednesday meetings."

"You're mean."

"You're right," Maxine agreed. "There's iced tea in the fridge."

"I don't like iced tea."

"I don't care."

"Fine." Dan turned and carried his glass to the refrigerator. He filled it with iced tea and took a big gulp. "What the Christ! There's no sugar in it."

Maxine walked in behind him. "It's unsweetened."

"Obviously."

"Get used to it. You don't need all that sugar either."

Dan walked toward the back door. "I want a divorce."

"Too bad. We're not married yet."

"Yeah, well … as soon as we are, I'm filing for divorce." Dan walked out and let the screen door slam behind him.

Chapter Five

Dan Coast sat in one of the dozen or so metal folding chairs in a conference room at the Big Pine Methodist Church. He had sat in that exact same spot a few times during the Monday AA meetings. He didn't know if it was the same chair, but they all felt pretty much the same to him—the cold hard metal feeling of defeat and shame. The conference room was bright white and had the sterile look of a hospital operating room. The three white ceiling fans spun slowly above the group. Dan stared up at the blades of one of the fans for a few seconds, and then returned his focus to the front of the room.

A pretty brunette about the same age as Dan—who Dan knew only as Ava—stood at the podium up front. "The judge ruled that I get to see my children every other weekend now," she announced. "So you could say it's been a pretty good week so far."

Ava had told the group already that it had been 331 days since her last drink. The group applauded that, and then applauded again as she returned to her chair. Ava smiled at Dan before turning and taking her seat in front of him.

Dan wondered if Ava would nag him about his drinking as much as Maxine did. Probably more, he figured, given the circumstances.

Hal, the AA chapter chair, walked up to the podium and asked if anyone else would like to share. Dan looked around the room. It looked like Ava would be the last. Hal cast an encouraging glance at Dan, but Dan wasn't about to broadcast his shortcomings and triumphs to this gathering of touchy-feely strangers. Dan had spoken out only a couple times-parroting bilge he'd heard the other members spout, just to appease Hal and Maxine.

As most of the group filed out, Dan stayed and helped fold and stack the chairs. When the task was complete, he walked over to a banquet table where there was a coffee maker, and poured himself some coffee into a Styrofoam to-go cup. He blew into the cup, took a sip, and placed a plastic lid on top.

Ava met Dan at the table and poured herself a cup as well. "I've missed you at the Monday meetings, Rick," she said.

Dan grinned, remembering he had always told everyone at the meetings that his name was Rick. "My name's not Rick," he confessed.

Ava looked confused. "I thought you—"

"I just use that name here," he explained. "I don't know why. Stupid, I guess."

"No," said Ava. "I understand."

Dan offered his hand. "Dan Coast."

Ava took his hand and gave it a slight shake. "Ava Mills."

"Sounds like everything is going real good for you," Dan said.

Ava nodded. "Yes, it is," she said. "I even got my old job back two weeks ago."

"That's great. What do you do?"

"I work in the office at Bayside Realty up in Marathon." A shameful look crossed her face. "They always treated me good … even when I wasn't treating them very good."

"They sound like good people." *Good*, Dan thought, *we're saying good a lot.*

Ava pulled a business card out of her purse and handed it to Dan. "So, if you're ever in the market for a new home … or anything else, give me a call." She smiled. Her teeth were just the right color of white, and perfectly straight.

Dan looked at the card. "I'll be sure to call you," he said. "I mean, if I'm ever, you know, in the market." Dan felt his face flush.

Ava smiled again. "Well, goodbye, Dan."

"Bye," Dan said. He pulled the lid off his cup and took another sip; it was still too hot. He put the lid back on.

"How's it going, Rick?" Hal asked, on his way by. He stopped and added: "Wish you'd share more with the group. Maybe next time?"

"Yeah, Hal, maybe next time," Dan replied. He faked a smile that made him look like the Grinch when he had a wonderful awful idea.

Hal clapped him on the back heartily, "That's the spirit."

Chapter Six

As Dan zipped along A1A in his Porsche, he reached into the side pocket of his cargo shorts and grabbed his cell phone. He turned it on and laid it in the passenger seat. It illuminated and buzzed a few times.

I should have grabbed a couple donuts, he thought.

Dan knew the Galley Grill would be coming up on the left. He thought back to last time he ate at the funky eatery with the to-die-for menu. He remembered the shootout there with Melvin Jessup, the redheaded hit man. Dan wondered if anyone at the Galley Grill would remember him. He wondered if he should stop and grab something to eat.

Maxine was already at work, so she wouldn't be at home to make him anything, and he was too lazy to make something for himself. He knew there was a box of unfrosted Pop-Tarts—the only good type of Pop-Tarts—in the cupboard, but he was hungrier than that.

His cell phone rang.

"Hello?"

"I've called you five times!" Red said.

"Including this call?" Dan asked.

"What?"

"Five times including this one, or five plus this one?"

"Including—what? I don't know. Shut up."

"What did you want?"

"Did you forget we were supposed to pick up your brother last night?"

"Sorry. Maxine wouldn't let me come out and play."

"You're pathetic."

"Ouch."

"Don't worry, I picked him up."

"I wasn't worried."

"He stayed at my house last night."

"Cool."

"Did you talk to your dad?"

"No. He won't be home until later tonight."

"Did you say anything to your mom?"

"Christ, no!"

"Where are you?"

"Just coming into Summerland Key."

"Did you eat breakfast?"

"No."

"Call Maxine and ask her if you can have breakfast with us."

"I don't need her permission."

"Do you want me to call her and ask?"

"I said I don't need her permission," Dan snapped back.

"Says the guy who couldn't leave his house last night."

"I could have."

"Then why didn't you?"

"Why don't you shut up? I'll be to your house in about a half hour."

"Okay, we'll wait for you, but hurry up."

"I said a half hour."

"But you're driving a Porsche, it should take only twenty—"

Dan hung up before Red could finish his sentence.

*****

Dan arrived on Thompson Street twenty-five minutes later and parked in front of Red's house. He climbed out of his car, walked across the street, and went inside.

Red and Richard Bong sat at Red's kitchen table, each with a cup of coffee in front of them.

Red looked up at the wall clock that hung above the table. "About time," he said.

"Morning, Dan," said Richard.

"Morning, Richard," Dan replied. "If that's your real name."

Richard managed a chuckle. Red's been telling me what a joker you are."

"I wasn't joking."

"You want a cup of coffee, Dan?" Red asked.

"Had three cups this morning already," Dan answered. "I just gotta get something to eat. I'm starving."

Red downed the remainder of his coffee. "Let's go then."

Dan wanted to ride to breakfast in his own car, but Red suggested they all ride over together in Richard's roomy Passat. Red let Dan ride up front with his "brother."

"So, Red tells me you're a private investigator," said Richard.

"Kinda," Dan replied.

"Don't be so modest," Red said from the backseat. He slapped his friend on the shoulder. "Me and Dan have solved quite a few cases over the last three years, or so."

"Oh yeah?" Richard said. "That sounds pretty cool."

"Tell him, Dan," Red prodded. "We solved a couple murders, some insurance fraud cases. We caught a couple cheating husbands. We even rescued a little Cuban girl from her kidnappers once. Got a citation and everything for that one. Tell him, Dan."

"You just told him, Red," said Dan. "What else did he tell you about me?"

"He mentioned you're getting married," Richard replied. "He told me you moved down here about five years ago with your dog."

"That's it?" Dan asked. He stared at Richard, waiting for the rest of Red's CliffsNotes version of his life story to be divulged.

"He didn't tell me you had won the lottery, if that's what—"

"There it is," said Dan.

"I didn't say anything," Red asserted.

"I found out myself, while I was looking for you," Richard said. "I stumbled upon a Dan Coast whose name was listed in a database of people who had won sizeable lottery jackpots in New York State. Naturally my curiosity kicked in and I followed up on it."

"And that's why you decided to track me down," Dan surmised.

"I was *tracking you down* before I found out about it," Richard explained. "I don't want any of your money, Dan."

"Well that's reassuring, brother," Dan said with much sarcasm.

Richard pulled the car to the curb on Eaton Street, in front of Endless Summer Apparel, and put it in park. He turned to Dan. "Listen, Coast, I don't want anything from you. I was an only child. The man I thought was my father passed away. After that, it was only me and my mother. Now that she's gone too, and I'm all alone. I just wanted to find you, meet you, and maybe spend some time getting to know you and the rest of my family. That's it. If this is too much for you, or you don't trust me, just give me the word and I'll be on the next plane outta here. But let me make one thing clear. Either way, I will be contacting our father. I need to meet him."

Dan stared at Richard without expression. He was silent.

"What's it gonna be, Coast?" Richard asked. "You want me to stay, or do you want me to leave?"

Dan slowly turned his head and looked out the front windshield. "We might as well get something to eat first."

Richard put the car back in drive and headed down Eaton Street.

"You're gonna want to make a right up here on Grinnell Street," said Dan.

Chapter Seven

"I'll have two eggs over-medium, home fries, bacon, and white toast," Dan said. He folded his menu and handed it to the waitress.

"I'll have the same," said Red, "but make my eggs scrambled, and I'll have rye toast instead of white. Also, sausage instead of bacon."

The waitress looked a little confused, but jotted it down anyway.

"How is that the same thing?" Dan asked, shaking his head.

"Eggs, meat, and toast," Red replied. "The same as you."

Richard chuckled. "I'll have the short stack of pancakes with sausage," he said.

"Thank you, gentlemen," said the young brunette. "I'll put that right in."

"Can I get some more coffee too?" Red asked.

"You sure can, hon," she replied.

Red watched the attractive twenty-something walk back to the kitchen. When she disappeared through the door he turned back to his companions. "She wants me," he said.

Dan snorted contemptuously. "Oh yeah, sure. What makes you say that?"

"She called me hon," Red replied.

"She probably calls everyone hon," said Richard.

"Did she call you hon?" Red asked.

"Well, no."

"Okay then. Besides, I'm sure you saw the look she gave me."

"What look was that?" Dan asked.

"You know ... the look."

"I don't know."

"I don't know either," Richard said. "You'll have to explain."

"The look," Red insisted.

"Can you demonstrate?" Richard asked.

Dan snickered. "Yeah, Red. Give Richard the look."

Red cocked his head slightly, tried his hardest to bat his eyelashes, and then gave his best come hither look. He gave a little pout and then an almost imperceptible nod of the head.

"Ohhh," said Richard. "The look."

"See what I mean?" Red said.

"No," Richard replied. "I didn't see her do that."

Dan laughed.

"Well, she did," said Red.

"We'll just have to take your word for it," Dan said.

"Screw both of you," Red mumbled.

"You give me *the look* one more time and I just might let you," Richard shot back.

Dan did a spit take. He and Richard couldn't stop laughing. Dan still had his suspicions, but he found himself warming up to the long-lost "brother."

Red got up from the table. "Laugh it up," he said. "I gotta piss."

Richard watched as the big man made his way toward the restroom. "How long you two been friends?" he asked.

"Since the first week I arrived, I guess. His place was the first bar I went to when I moved here."

"What made you pick his place?"

"It was one of the only places my wife and I hadn't—" Dan paused. He moved his coffee cup an inch to the left, and straitened his silverware on the napkin. He needed a second to continue. "It was one of the only places my wife and I hadn't been to together."

"Red told me you lost your wife right before you moved down here."

"Yeah, that's right, but the two of us came down here for a couple weeks right before she passed away."

"I see."

"We purchased the house where I now live. We returned home—upstate New York—to pack our things for the move down here. She was killed in an automobile accident a few days before the move."

"I'm sorry," Richard said.

"Thanks."

"You also had a brother that passed when you were kids."

Dan nodded. "Yes."

"How did that happen?"

"I'd rather not talk about that … Rich." Dan looked around the room for the waitress. When he made eye contact, he raised his coffee mug. She nodded her head, and went for the coffee maker.

"Yeah, okay."

The two men sat in silence until after the waitress arrived and refilled their mugs.

"Red says you're getting married," Richard said.

"Yup."

"Have a date set?"

"Not yet, but don't bring that up when you meet Maxine. It's kind of a sore subject."

"I was hoping I would get to meet her."

"How about later this evening?" Dan suggested.

"That would be great," Richard replied excitedly. "How about if I take the two of you out for dinner?"

"Why don't we just meet you at Red's around six," Dan suggested. "We'll eat there. Red can give you directions to the place."

"Sounds good."

The two men turned their heads and watched as the big bow-legged man returned from the bathroom.

"Miss me?" Red asked.

"Like a big turd after the flush," Dan replied.

Chapter Eight

After breakfast, Richard dropped Dan back off at Red's house. Dan climbed into his car and headed straight for the Key West Police Department.

"I need a favor, Rick," Dan said. He sat in one of the two wooden chairs facing Chief of Police Rick Carver's desk. Sitting on top of Rick's desk was a half-eaten Cuban Mix sandwich (a deliciously artery-hardening medley of ham, cheese, roast pork, salami, lettuce, tomatoes, and pickles) from the Key West Corner Sandwich Shop, and a Diet Pepsi.

Rick looked at Dan for a few seconds without saying anything. Dan noticed that Rick's lips were moving, like he was talking silently to himself. Finally Rick leaned back in his chair and spoke. "You know, Coast, I needed a favor from you last week, but you didn't deliver." Rick didn't seem angry, nor was he speaking as loud as he usually did. He seemed calm.

"What favor was that, Rick?" Dan asked.

"When you and I found that body upstairs in the house next door to yours."

"At the Stewarts' place?"

"Yes," Rick replied. "Do you remember the one thing I asked of you?"

"Keep my nose out of it?"

"Exactly."

"But, Rick, we—"

Rick put up his hand to silence his friend. "There's no but. I asked you to stay out of it, but you wouldn't listen."

"And we solved the case," Dan reminded him.

"That's beside the point. My therapist says that if you and I can't get on the same page as far as our relationship goes, then I can no longer stay in this relationship. It's just not healthy for me."

"Relationship?" Dan asked.

"Yes."

"Same page?"

"The same page."

"Therapist? What therapist?"

"I've been seeing a therapist for about a month now. She helps me with my anger issues. I've been off my blood pressure medication for over a week now."

"Um … that's great. Are you also on drugs? Because you seem like you're on drugs. Something just doesn't seem right with you lately."

Rick cocked his head and looked pitifully at his friend. "Everything has never been more right."

"Okay. So then, you're going to do me the favor?"

"Of course I am. That's what friends are for. But I expect the same respect from you from this point on. Do I have your word?"

"Of course, Rick."

"Now what's the favor?"

"Someone claiming to be my brother showed up in town the other day."

"I didn't know you had a brother."

"Neither did I. He says my father and his mother were together in Vietnam. He and his mother, along with the man he thought was his father, moved to the states when he was young. Before his mother passed away, she told him the truth about his birth father."

"I see. Have you spoken to your dad about this?"

"I called him, but he's out of town and won't be back until tonight. He's supposed to call me back when he gets home."

"And you want me to run a check on this guy." Rick pulled a note pad over in front of him and picked up a pencil. "What's his name?"

"He says his name is Richard Bong, and he's from Texas. He says he's forty-six years old. His mother's name was Tran—maiden name Pham—and his adoptive father's name was Kim. That's all I know about him."

Rick jotted as Dan spoke. When he finished writing, he lay the pencil down on top of the notepad. "That should be enough to go on," he said. "I'll let you know what I find out."

"Thanks," Dan said, as he stood up from the chair. He looked down at the half-eaten Cuban sandwich. Then his eyes went to Rick's huge gut. "Is your therapist going to help you with—never mind."

"Help me with what?" Rick asked.

"Nothing," Dan answered. He turned and grabbed the doorknob.

"Oh, and Dan, the therapist thing, that's just between you and me. I don't really want it getting out that I'm seeing a therapist."

"Of course, Rick. I promise I won't say a word."

"Thanks, Dan."

"No problem, pal." Dan turned and went out the door. As he was crossing the parking lot toward his car he reached for his cell phone and dialed.

"Hello?" said Red.

"Rick's seeing a friggin' therapist."

Chapter Nine

"I can't believe Rick is seeing a therapist," said Maxine.

"I know," Dan agreed. "I was just as shocked as you."

"Do you know who it is?"

"I have no idea. But don't mention it to anyone. He asked me not to say anything."

"Oh, I wouldn't say anything."

"Red said he wouldn't say anything either."

"You told Red?"

"Well, yeah."

"I'm nervous," Maxine said, as Dan steered the car into the parking lot of Red's Bar and Grill.

Dan put the Porsche in reverse and backed into a spot across the lot next to the picnic tables. "Nervous about what?" he asked.

"About meeting your brother," she replied.

Dan shut off the engine and turned to Maxine. "Listen, we don't even know if he really is my brother. Just because he says he is, doesn't mean he is."

"Why would he lie about it?' Maxine scoffed.

"Money!" Dan replied. "He wants money."

Maxine started to open the door but paused. "I've never asked you this before, but exactly how much money are you worth?"

"It doesn't matter."

"Hundreds of thousands?"

"Really, it doesn't matter."

"Millions?"

"Maxine."

"Hundreds of millions?"

Dan didn't answer.

"Billions?"

"Dan opened his door. "Let's go meet my *brother*," he said, putting finger quotes around the word brother.

"Someday you'll have to tell me how much money."

Dan continued to walk toward the entrance of the bar.

"I'm going to be your wife, pal."

Dan said nothing.

"If we ever set a date," said Maxine.

Dan pulled open the door and held it for Maxine.

"Am I in your will at least?" asked Maxine.

Dan continued to ignore her.

"Am I going to have to sign a prenup?"

These were all questions that Maxine really didn't care about, but ribbing her future husband was fun.

Dan entered behind Maxine and let the door close behind him. He spotted Richard at the bar. He was sitting on Dan's favorite stool. There were six other empty stools.

"What the Christ?" Dan grumbled. *Sitting on my stool.*

Richard turned when he heard the footsteps behind him. "Hey," he said.

"Hey," Dan responded.

Maxine stepped up beside Dan. She smiled at Richard. "You must be Richard," she said.

Richard slid off the stool and offered his hand. "That's me," he said. "And you must be Maxine."

Maxine didn't shake Richard's hand. Instead, she went in for a hug.

"Oh," said Richard surprised, "you're a hugger."

"Well, you're family."

Dan rolled his eyes. *Family*, he thought.

Richard picked up his glass. "Shall we get a table?" he asked.

Dan made eye contact with Cindy behind the bar. "Tequila, Seven, and lime," he ordered.

"Comin' right up," Cindy said.

"Put that on *my* tab," said Richard.

Big spender, Dan thought. "Thanks."

The three made their way across the room to a four-top near the jukebox and sat. A minute later, Cindy arrived with Dan's drink, and a Michelob Ultra for Maxine.

"Thanks," said Maxine.

"Abby will be right over to take your order," Cindy informed them.

"Abby?" Dan asked.

"Red hired her this morning," Cindy said. "Maxine recommended her for the job."

Dan gave Maxine a puzzled look. "She did?" he asked. "Who's Abby?"

"She's Colton's girlfriend," Maxine replied. "She told me she was looking for a job, and I told her she should try here."

"Well, wasn't that nice of you." said Dan sarcastically. "How did you even meet Colton's girlfriend?"

"She stopped by the house on Monday to see Colton. I was outside with Bev—"

"Gawking at Colton?" Dan threw in.

"No," Maxine argued defensively. "We were just standing out front talking."

"Because you always stand out front talking."

"Can I finish?"

"I guess."

"Anyway, he introduced us to Abby."

"And you told her to get a job."

Richard snickered.

"No. She told us she was looking for a job."

"And you told her about Red's."

"Is that a problem?'

"If she works here, now *he'll* be hanging around all the time."

"What's wrong with that?"

"I don't like staring at him all the time like some people I could name."

"Then don't."

"I mean, I don't think he's as pretty as you."

"I hope not," said Maxine. "I'm much prettier."

"That's not what I mean. I don't think he's as pretty as you think he is."

"Why don't you quit while you're not too far behind?" Richard suggested.

"Yeah, good idea," Dan agreed.

"Good evening," said the twenty-something red head. "My name is Abby and I'll be taking care of you this— hey, Maxine!"

"Hi, Abby! How are you liking the new job?"

"So far so good."

Maxine introduced Abby to Dan and Richard and gave her the Reader's Digest version of their long-lost brother's story. Dan sat quietly wondering why Maxine thought anyone would want to hear about it.

When Maxine finished the story, Abby took their orders and went to the kitchen.

"You don't have to tell everybody you meet our life story," said Dan.

"Life story?" Maxine shot back. "I wouldn't call that your life story." She turned to Richard. "So, Richard, what do you do in Texas?"

"I own a little pharmacy in a small community called Port Arthur. It's on the western shore of Sabine Lake, a huge estuary on the Louisiana-Texas border. Beautiful place. My father purchased the store in 1980."

"That's where you live, Port Arthur?"

"I actually live about an hour away, in Caplen, Texas."

"That's quite a commute," said Dan.

"It's not too bad. I only work at the store two or three days a week now."

"You're a pharmacist?" asked Maxine.

"Yes, but since my father passed, and I took over the store, I've cut my hours back quite a bit."

"What do you do in your spare time?" Maxine asked.

Richard chuckled. "Not much. I surf a little. I play drums in a band. We play area bars a couple nights a week. I'm pretty much semi-retired."

"No wife?" Dan asked.

Richard shook his head. "Nope."

"Girlfriend?" asked Maxine.

"I have a dog. His name is Buddy."

"Oh my God!" said Maxine.

"What?" asked Richard.

"Dan's dog's name is Buddy."

Richard looked at Dan. "Are you serious?"

"Dan nodded. "Yes. He's a border collie lab mix."

"My dog is a beagle," said Richard. "But how crazy is it that they have the same name?"

"Crazy," Dan agreed half-heartedly.

"I've heard of things like that before," said Maxine. "I heard about these brothers who were given up for adoption at birth. When they found each other in their forties, they were both cops, both had wives with the same first name, and both had three children."

"We're only half-brothers," said Dan, "so it's probably just the dog thing."

"You never know," Maxine said. "What's your favorite color, Richard?"

"Blue, I guess."

"What's yours, Dan?"

"You don't know my favorite color?" Dan asked.

"No."

Dan humphed. "And you want to be in my will."

"Well, what is it?" Maxine pressed.

"I don't have a favorite color."

"Everyone has a favorite color," Maxine insisted.

"I don't," Dan argued.

"That's weird."

"Is it?" Dan asked. "I don't think it is."

"Steak and mashed potatoes?" Abby asked.

"Right here," said Dan. "And can I get another drink?"

Abby sat Dan's plate in front of him. "You sure can," she said. She placed Maxine and Richard's plates in front of them. "Can I get either of you two another drink?"

"I'm good," said Maxine.

"I'll take another," said Richard.

Abby returned a few minutes later, and a few minutes after that, Red bounded through the kitchen door.

"No one told me you guys were here!" said Red.

"We tipped extra for that," Dan said.

"Very funny." Red pulled out a chair and took a seat at the table. He looked toward the bar. "Cindy!" he shouted. "Scotch on the rocks!"

"Please!" Cindy shouted back.

"Please." Red said. He turned back to Dan. "So, what time we leavin' in the mornin'?"

"I don't know," Dan replied. "It's what, about a four and a half hour drive?"

"Give or take," said Red.

"Let's leave at six thirty. That'll give us time to look around before Maggie gets to the restaurant. I wanted to swing by her father's house first and get a look at the place."

"Sounds good," said Red. "Six thirty sound okay with you, Rich?"

"Fine with me," Richard answered.

"Wait … what?" Dan asked.

"I invited Rich along," said Red. "We decided to take his Passat. There's more room for all of us."

"You decided?" Dan asked.

"I didn't think you would mind," Red said.

Richard said, "If you don't want me to go—"

"No, that's fine," said Dan.

Red looked around the room. "How come nobody is playing the jukebox?" He stood up and reached into his pocket for some change. "What kind of music do you like, Rich?"

"I'm a pretty big Buffett fan," Rich said.

"Ha!" Maxine shouted. "He's a big Buffett fan! Just like you, Dan."

"One of the most popular entertainers of the last forty years. What are the odds?" Dan deadpanned.

Chapter Ten

By seven o'clock Red and Richard had picked up Dan and the three men were headed north on A1A in Richard's Volkswagen Passat, just outside of Summerland Key. The radio was tuned to Radio Margaritaville, and Dan tapped his thigh with his thumb to the beat of "Surfing in a Hurricane." He was wearing his RayBan Wayfarers, but still squinting as he gazed out over the water.

"The Galley Grill is right up here on the right," Red said matter-of-factly, from the backseat.

"So what?" Dan responded.

"Gettin' kinda hungry."

"Didn't you eat before you picked me up?"

"No."

"Why not?"

"We usually stop on the way."

"Usually? When was the last time we drove up to West Palm Beach together?'

"I don't think we ever did."

"Then how can there be a usually?"

"I'm getting a little hungry too," said Richard.

"Of course you are," said Dan. He reached up and turned the music down a bit.

"Turn right up here, Rich" said Red.

Richard steered his car off the road and into the parking lot of the Galley Grill. The three men climbed out of the car and walked up the concrete ramp, and through a doorway to the outside dining area. They waited at the door for the hostess.

A waitress saw them and said, "You can sit anywhere you like."

The trio grabbed a booth against the lattice wall that surrounded the patio. The waitress who had spoken to them soon arrived at the table with a coffee pot in her hand.

"Coffee for everyone?" she asked.

"Yes," they all said.

She poured the coffee and when she got to Dan she stared for a second. "Do I know you?" she asked.

"I don't think so," Dan said.

"You look familiar."

"Everyone says that."

"You ready to order?"

"Yes."

"I need a second," Red said.

"No you don't," Dan said. "I'll have two eggs over medium, bacon, and white toast."

Richard said, "I'll have the same thing."

The waitress looked at Red.

"I don't know what I want."

"Come on," said Dan. "She hasn't got all day."

"Just bring me the same thing," said Red. "But scrambled eggs, and rye instead of white."

"Jesus Christ!" Dan said.

"Well, ya got me all flustered."

"How could you be flustered? You've ordered breakfast before."

"But I didn't know what I wanted."

"How can you not know what you want for breakfast?" Dan scolded. "They probably haven't invented anything new for breakfast since the Egg McMuffin, and we ain't at McDonald's. There's eggs, meat, bread, pancakes, and French toast. That's it."

"I can't decide that quickly."

"I knew what I wanted the second we pulled into the parking lot."

"Well you're just weird," Red said. "I heard you don't even have a favorite color."

"Oh shut up."

Richard was trying his best not to laugh. "Sorry, Dan, I told him about the favorite color thing."

"Whatever. It doesn't matter."

The waitress returned a few minutes later. As she set their plates in front of them, she stared at Dan. "I'll think of it," she said.

"I hope you do," Dan replied.

When the waitress walked away, Red said, "Dan was in a shootout here awhile back."

Richard's eyes widened. "A shootout? Like … a real shootout?"

Dan nodded, and took a sip of his coffee. "Yup," he said. "A real shootout."

"What happened?" Richard asked.

As the three men ate their breakfast Dan told Richard about Lance Beacon, and how he hired a hitman and put out contract on his own life. He and Red talked about the red headed hit man that jumped through Dan's window and ended up being shot in the parking lot of a burning hotel. Richard remained enthralled with the story from beginning to end.

"Wow," Richard said. "That. Is. Awesome!"

Dan was pretty proud of himself, and the fact that his big brother thought he was so cool.

"Yeah, all in a day's work," said Red. He leaned back in his chair and stretched his arms over his head.

Dan downed the last of his coffee. "Let's get back on the road."

The waitress hurried toward them. She was pointing her finger at Dan. "You were here a few weeks back," she recalled. "Now I remember. You and that other guy. You were almost killed out front when that maniac opened fire with his gun."

Dan nodded. "That's me." He glanced over at Richard. Richard had a big grin on his face. At that moment Dan liked having a brother. It had been a long time since he had felt that way.

Chapter Eleven

At Eleven fifteen Richard Bong took a right off of Cocoanut Row onto Clarke Avenue. He, Dan, and Red were enroute to E.R. Bradley's for their lunch date with Maggie Harrison, as planned, they took a detour to check out the estate of her father, Harrison Harrison, the mouthpiece so nice, they named him twice.

"This is the street Maggie's father lives on?" Red asked.

"According to Google," Dan answered. "Should be at the end here, on the right." He pointed down the street.

"Harrison Harrison must be a *very* successful attorney," said Richard, gazing in awe at the brick and stucco mansions as they drove along the palm tree-lined street.

"I guess so," Dan agreed.

"I want a house like this," said Red.

"Go to law school," Richard responded.

When they got to the corner of Clarke Avenue and South County Road, Richard stopped at the stop sign. They all three looked to their right, past the gated driveway, at the huge brick home.

"It looks like the Playboy Mansion," said Red.

"I wonder if there's any Playmates inside?" Richard deadpanned.

Two security guards in black three-piece suits stood at the gate. The massive guards stared at Richard's car with blank expressions. Their hands were folded at the waist. When Richard made eye contact with one of the men, he realized he had been sitting at the stop sign just a little too long, and drove on through the intersection.

"What do you think Tweedledee and Tweedledum are for?" Dan asked, referring to the security guards.

"I don't know," Richard replied. "My attorney doesn't have any guards."

"Mine neither," Red said.

"Your attorney doesn't even have an office, Red," said Dan.

"He does too," Red argued.

"A storage unit is not an office."

"Where to?" Richard asked.

"Take a right up here, and circle back around," Dan responded. "Let's get a look at the back of the place."

"I wonder if he has a pool?" Red mused.

"I bet he has a real nice pool," said Richard.

Richard took a right onto South Ocean Boulevard and then a right onto Seabreeze Avenue. He drove up one block and stopped at the stop sign.

"Turn right," Dan said, "and then we'll take a left into the alley."

"You want me to drive down the alley?" Richard asked nervously.

"Yeah, why not?"

"What if there's not an outlet, and we're stuck in there? What if the guards notice the car?"

"You sound scared, Richard," Dan observed.

"Not scared, just cautious."

Richard pulled into the narrow alley, barely wide enough for two cars to pass each other. It was shady due to the many overhanging palm fronds and tree branches. Two black Lincoln Navigators with tinted windows were park at the rear entrance to the Harrison home. Three other guards stood near the rear gate and the two Navigators. The three tough guys were dressed identical to the ones out front.

"Wow," Richard whispered.

"Yeah," Dan agreed. "This guy does something other than practice law."

"Look at that pool," said Red. "It's the size of a small lake."

Richard continued down the alley cautiously. He came to a stop at Cocoanut Row. "Which way?" he asked.

Dan fumbled for his phone. "Hold on," he said. "Let me see where this place is." He tapped the Google Maps icon and entered E.R. Bradley's. "Take a right."

As Richard went slowly around the corner, Dan glanced back down the alley. One of the guards was standing in the middle of the alley watching them. His hands were on his hips. Dan felt a cold chill run down his spine.

"You think my yard is big enough for a pool?" Red asked.

"Please shut up about the pool," said Dan. "Take a left up here on Royal Poinciana Way."

Richard took the left and headed over the Flagler Memorial Bridge.

"Take a left at the end of the bridge," Dan instructed.

"Are we almost there?" Red asked.

"We're two minutes away," Dan said. "Calm down."

"I'm starving."

"Of course you are."

"Oh, forgive me," Red shot back. "How about if I don't talk about swimming pools *or* food."

"That's a good start."

"You're a dick."

"Boys, boys," said Richard. "Play nice or I'll turn this car around."

Chapter Twelve

Arriving at E.R. Bradley's, Dan, Red, and Richard walked up the concrete steps toward the outside bar that sat under a massive green vinyl canopy. Dan scanned the outdoor seating area to his left.

"Three of you?" asked the tall thin hostess. She wore a black golf shirt with the buttons undone, and a pair of black shorts. Her gold name tag said TAMMY. Her long blonde hair was pulled back in a ponytail.

"We're meeting someone," Dan replied. His eyes settled on a young woman he recognized. "There she is."

"Okay," said Tammy. "You can have a seat and I'll bring some menus right over."

The three men walked toward a round table underneath a giant thatched umbrella. Maggie Harrison recognized Dan right away and smiled like she was seeing an old friend.

"Mr. Coast, I'm so glad to see you!" She stood and hugged him. Recognizing Red, she hugged him as well.

She looked at Richard. "You weren't with them that night at the hotel."

"No," Richard explained. "I'm Richard Bong, a … uh, friend of Dan and Red's"

Maggie and Richard shook hands.

"It's nice to meet you," said Maggie. "Everyone sit down, please."

The men sat and a waitress soon arrived. She took their drink order and told them she would be right back.

The outside dining area of E.R. Bradley's was on the opposite side of Flagler Drive, and over-looked the Intracoastal Waterway.

"I was expecting a more private, out of the way meeting spot," Dan said.

"I thought it would be better to meet out in the open at a crowded, public place," Maggie responded.

"Why's that?" Red asked.

"Just in case," said Maggie.

"Just in case of what?" Dan asked.

"You never know," Maggie replied.

The three men all looked at each other. Dan could see that Richard was a little nervous. He figured it was because Richard was a lot smarter than him and Red.

"Maggie, that's a little vague," Dan said. "What are you afraid might happen?"

Maggie looked around the restaurant. "Well, it's like I told you, I think my father killed my mother and is blaming it on my boyfriend."

"Your boyfriend, Steve," said Red. "The guy we met at the hotel in Haines City."

"Yes."

"What makes you think it was your father?" Dan asked.

Maggie reached into her pocket book that was sitting on the floor next to her chair. She pulled out her cell phone and placed it on the table in front of her. "Because of a conversation I heard the night the police brought me home." Maggie slid the phone across the table to Dan. "I recorded the whole thing."

Dan stared at the phone for a second and then pushed it back across the table. "Listen, Maggie, I have to be honest with you. I'm not a *real* private investigator. I have no license to do this sort of thing."

"Just listen to the recording," Maggie insisted.

"I don't want to."

Red picked up the cell. "Well I want to hear it."

"Put it down, Red," Dan ordered.

"You're not the boss of me." Red pushed a button on the back of the cell and it lit up. "How do I listen to this thing?"

Maggie took the phone from him and opened the recording app. "Just hit the play button," she said, handing it back to him. "Just not too loud."

Red hit the play button and there was a few seconds of bumping and static. Then a man's voice came on. "I don't want that little bastard to make to trial. You understand me?"

A second man said, "Yes, sir, Mr. Harrison. I understand."

"Where is he now?" asked the first man.

"He's in the Haines City lock up. He'll be brought to the West Palm PD sometime tomorrow and processed.

After that, he'll be taken to the Palm Beach County Detention Center."

"We have someone inside there?"

"Yes."

"Tell him to do it quick. There's no reason for the little shit to suffer."

"Yes, sir."

"Get that taken care of, and we'll only have one more to go."

"Yes, sir."

There was another bumping sound.

"Did you hear that?" asked the first guy. "Check out in the hall."

The recording stopped. Red sat the phone back down on the table.

"That's when I turned it off and ran to my room," said Maggie.

"No one else knows about that recording?" Dan asked.

Maggie shook her head. "No one."

"I really don't think we can help you," Dan said.

Maggie's eyes began to tear up. "Why not?" she asked. "In Haines City you told me if there was anything I needed, just to call you."

"But I didn't know it was something like this."

Red and Richard remained silent. Dan knew they both felt terrible, but he also knew they both agreed with him.

"The only people who can help you are the police," Dan advised. "There's nothing I can do. It's not like on television, or in cheap mystery books, Maggie. Regular people like us don't take on something like this."

"We drove by your house before we came here, Maggie," said Red. "We saw the armed guards. It's obvious your dad is more than just a lawyer. We can't go up against people like that."

"You're scared," Maggie surmised.

"Damn right we're scared," said Dan. "Mostly we take pictures of cheating husbands, and find missing people. We've caught a few murderers, but most of them were just regular people, not guys like your dad."

"And when we got into something really bad," Red explained, "it wasn't by choice. It was usually by accident."

Maggie slumped back in her chair, and sighed. "I understand … I guess," she said defeatedly.

Red picked up her phone and handed it to her. "Go to the police."

"Okay," she said, taking the phone.

The waitress returned and asked, "Are you ready to order?"

"I don't think we'll be eating," Dan replied. "I'll just take another drink."

"What?" Red asked. "We're not eating?"

"We won't be here that long," Dan replied.

"Give me another drink too," said Red.

"I'm good," said Richard.

The waitress looked at Maggie. "Miss?" Maggie shook her head.

The waitress headed back to the bar.

"Well if no one else is going to ask, I will," said Richard. "Why would your father kill your mother, and why would he want you dead?"

Dan shook his head in disapproval. He didn't want to know anything else about the girl's situation. He knew the more he heard the worse he would feel later for not taking the case.

"Money?" said Maggie, as though she wasn't too sure.

"Your father doesn't look like he's hurting for money," said Richard.

"Well, no, but maybe—"

"This is for the police to determine," Dan said.

"I know," said Richard, "but there must be a reason she thinks her own father would want her dead. I mean, it's not normal that a kid would think their parent wanted to kill them."

"He said 'two down, one to go.' I'm the one," said Maggie.

"How do you know that?" asked Red. "Maybe Steve *did* kill your mom, and now your dad wants to get even. I know I would."

"Why would Steve kill my mom?" Maggie asked.

"Who knows?" said Dan. "But to us it's no more far-fetched than your father wanting to kill you. I don't know what's going on, and I don't want to."

Maggie picked up her phone and tossed it back into her pocketbook. "Fine," she said. "Don't believe me. I'll just end up dead, and it'll be all your fault." She stood up. "You'll see."

Maggie turned and stormed across the patio and down the steps to the street. The three men watched until she disappeared around the corner.

The waitress returned and sat their drinks on the table. Dan grabbed his and downed half the glass.

"I hope we did the right thing," said Red.

"Yeah, me too," said Dan.

"I should have got another drink," Richard said.

"You're the designated driver," Dan reminded him.

"Oh yeah."

The guys sat there for another twenty-five minutes or so feeling bad for what they had just done. After they finished their drinks Dan slipped a hundred dollar bill into the check folder. As he was putting his money clip away, he felt his cell phone vibrate. He looked at the caller ID.

"Who is it?" Red asked.

"I have no idea." Dan laid the cell on the table.

"Shouldn't you answer it?" asked Richard.

"If it's important, they'll leave a message," said Dan.

The three men got up from the table and headed for the exit. They walked down the steps to Clematis Street and walked around the patio to Datura Street, where Richard had parked the car. Richard was first in line, then Red. Dan brought up the rear.

"We're gonna have to stop somewhere and eat," Red complained.

"Yeah, yeah," said Dan.

Suddenly Dan felt someone behind him. He started to turn around, but before he could, he felt the hard steel barrel of a .45 in his back. He knew what it was immediately.

"Do anything stupid and I'll split your spine," said the gunman.

"There should be a Wendy's around here somewhere," said Red obliviously.

The gunman grabbed Dan's shoulder with his left hand and steered him across the street. Out of the corner of his eye, Dan saw three other men. They were dressed like Harrison's guards. The three men hurried to catch up with Red and Richard.

Red sensed the movement behind him and spun around. He saw one of the men moving quickly toward him. Red swung a left, hitting the massive man in the right cheek. The man took a step back and shook it off as the third man pulled his weapon.

Red froze with his hands half in the air.

Richard spun around. His eyes widened. The fourth guard grabbed him by the front of the shirt and pulled him across the street and into a group of palm trees that sat between the Meyer Amphitheater and Datura Street.

With the third guard's gun in his back, Red hurried across the street, arms held high. The brute Red had hit followed, scowling and massaging his cheek.

The first guard shoved Dan up against a palm tree, and held him there with his forearm on Dan's throat.

"Did I not leave a big enough tip?" Dan wheezed.

"Shut up, asshole," said the brute. He turned to see where his cronies were.

Richard's man shoved him to his knees in the grass. Red's guy did the same to him. When the man Red hit reached the trees, he pulled out a chrome .44 revolver and smashed it against the side of Red's head. Red went limp and fell backwards into the grass.

"Jesus Christ!" Richard shouted.

The hulking gunman returned his weapon to its shoulder holster and wiped the blood from his cheek where

Red had split the man's skin. "One more word out of you," the gunman informed Richard, "and you'll get the same."

Dan's man returned his attention to Dan.

"What do you want?" Dan asked.

The man took out his weapon again and shoved the barrel up under Dan's chin. "Mr. Harrison wanted us to give you a message."

"An email would have been fine," Dan said. "You really didn't have to—"

He pushed the barrel harder into the soft tissue under Dan's chin, halting Dan's sarcasm.

Dan moved his eyes downward to see Richard on his knees with a gun to his temple. Richard looked more scared than Dan had ever seen anyone look. He could see his hands and shoulders trembling with fear.

"Go back to Key West," said the man, "and never set foot in West Palm Beach again. Never speak to Mr. Harrison's daughter again. If you do, we'll kill all three of you and dump your bodies where they'll never be found. You understand me?"

Dan nodded his head.

"Let me hear you say it."

"I … under … stand," Dan choked out.

The man with his gun to Richard's head looked down at Richard and said, "We're counting on you to help him keep his promise."

Richard nodded and dropped his head. He stared into the grass until he heard the four men walk away. When he finally heard four car doors shut, he sat back on his feet, put his face in his hands, and began to sob.

Dan's cell phone vibrated. "Hello?" he answered.

"Dan, it's Joey Pantucco. Get out of West Palm as quick as you can. There's some men coming for you."

"A little late, Joey," Dan said.

"I tried to call you sooner, but you didn't answer."

"Go figure," Dan said. "Thanks anyway, Joey. I'll call you back in a few hours." He hung up his cell and slipped it back into his pocket.

"So I take it the call *was* important," Richard sobbed.

Dan walked over and put his hand on Richard's shoulder. "Yeah, I guess I should have answered it."

"Ya ... think?"

Dan patted Richard's back. "Let it out, ya big wuss," he said. "You're shaking like a dog shittin' peach pits."

Chapter Thirteen

Richard decided to let Dan drive his rented Passat back to Key West. Dan agreed, since Richard's hands were still shaking so hard he couldn't grasp the steering wheel. Red lay in the back seat with a small bag of ice they had purchased at Walgreens pressed against the side of his head.

"How ya feelin', pal?" Dan asked.

Richard and Red both answered, "Fine."

Dan adjusted the rearview mirror to see Red. "Still bleeding?" he asked.

"No," Red replied.

Dan glanced over at Richard. Richard stared at the road ahead. "Havin' fun yet?" he asked.

"Just glad to be alive," Richard answered.

"That's a plus in most situations."

"Weren't you scared?" Richard asked.

"I almost shit my pants," Dan admitted. "I think I may have peed a little."

"You were making jokes."

"That's because I'm an idiot, not because I'm fearless."

"He's right," Red agreed. "He is an idiot."

"At least I didn't sleep through the whole ordeal," said Dan.

"At least I didn't piss myself," said Red.

"Barely any came out," Dan shot back. "It's already dry."

"You're both idiots," said Richard.

"Ouch," said Dan.

"So, what now?" asked Red.

"What do you mean?" Dan asked.

"What are we gonna do about Maggie Harrison?"

"I know you slept through the entire thing, but Harrison's goons made it pretty clear that we're to stay away from Maggie Harrison."

"It just seems like there's something we should do."

"Drop it." Dan's cell phone vibrated and he looked at the screen. "Unknown caller," Dan read aloud.

"Answer it!" Richard and Red shouted.

"Yeah, maybe I better," Dan agreed. "Hello?"

"Dan, it's Rick," said Chief Carver.

"Hey, what's up?"

"Can you talk?"

"Um, give me ten minutes and I'll call you right back."

"Sounds good."

"You in your office?"

"No, but I will be in ten minutes."

Dan hung up his cell and his eyes went to the roadside signs ahead. "There's a Wendy's right up here off the Saint Lucie Boulevard exit," he announced. "You want me to get off?"

"Yes," Red answered. "I'm starving."

"I don't know if I can eat yet," said Richard.

Dan flipped on his blinker and turned down the exit ramp. He took a left onto Saint Lucie Boulevard and pulled into the Wendy's parking lot.

"You guys go on in," said Dan. "I have to call Rick back."

"You got it," said Red. He climbed out of the back seat still holding the bag of ice. He bent over and looked at himself in the passenger-side mirror. "Shit. That's quite a lump." His right eye was starting to turn purple. He tossed the bag of ice back into the car through the open window, turned, and headed toward the entrance; Richard followed.

Dan stayed in the car and dialed Rick's number.

"Carver," Rick answered.

"Rick, it's Dan."

"I know. I got some information on your brother."

"Half-brother ... maybe."

"Can I continue?"

"I wish you would."

"His name is Richard G, Bong. I can't find anything that mentions his full middle name; just the G."

"It could stand for Gene, like my dad."

"I wondered about that myself. His story checks out. His parents are from North Vietnam. They did come to this country around the time he said they did. He is forty-six years old and he lives in Caplen, Texas. Caplen is an unincorporated community on what's called the Bolivar Peninsula in Galveston County. Richard lives in a very nice house right on the beach. The Bong family first settled in Houston, and a few years later they relocated to Port Arthur, where Kim worked at a local drug store. In the late seventies or early eighties, when the owner of the drug store retired, Kim Bong purchased the place."

"So it sounds like Richard was telling the truth about everything," said Dan.

"Yes, but get this, Kim didn't stop with one pharmacy."

"What do you mean?"

"Over the next twenty years, Kim Bong opened seven stores between Port Arthur and Houston. Richard still owns the place in Port Arthur, as well as stores in Winnie, Stowell, Wallisville, and a few other Texas burgs. From what I can tell, Richard is worth quite a bit of money."

"Huh," said Dan. "I wonder why he didn't mention that?"

"Who knows? Maybe he wanted to make sure you wouldn't want any first."

"Yeah, maybe," said Dan. "Thanks, Rick, I'll talk to ya later." Dan hung up his cell and went inside to get something to eat.

The young, skinny, pimple-faced kid behind the counter was just sliding Red his tray when Dan walked up to order. Richard had already brought his tray to a booth.

"That was Rick on the phone?" Red asked.

"Yes," Dan replied.

"Was he able to get any information on Rich?"

"Quite a bit, actually."

"Anything bad?"

"Nope."

"Did he lie about anything?"

"Let's just say, he didn't tell the *whole* truth."

"What do you mean?" Red and Dan stepped back away from the counter to let someone else order.

"Go ahead," Dan said to the elderly woman behind him.

"Thank you, young man," she said.

Dan returned his attention to Red. "Seems my big brother owns not one, but several pharmacies. According to Rick, he's loaded."

"That's good news. At least now you know he's not here for your money."

"I guess," said Dan.

Red turned and went to the booth where Richard was seated. Dan waited for the old woman to finish ordering, and then he stepped up to the counter.

"I'll have a double cheeseburger, medium fries, and a medium Coke," said Dan.

"Hold on a second," said the beanpole. He stared at the keyboard and punched a few buttons. "Okay, what?"

"I'll have a double cheeseburger, medium fries, and a medium Coke," Dan repeated.

The kid looked puzzled. He turned his head and stared at the menu display above him. "Double cheeseburger?" he asked.

"Yeah, double cheeseburger. It's twice the single cheeseburger."

"Uh … I don't think we have a double cheeseburger."

Dan pointed at the screen. "Right there … the double cheeseburger."

"Are you talking about the Dave's Double?"

"Yeah."

"Okay." The kid glanced back down at the cash register. "You want cheese on that?"

"You're asking me if I want cheese on my cheeseburger?"

"Well, do ya?"

"Yes."

"Will that be all?"

"I already told you—twice. Medium Coke and medium fries."

"Coke and fries. Medium?"

"Yes."

"Did you want chili or cheese on those?"

"Did I fuckin' say I wanted cheese or chili on them?"

The kid looked up at Dan with surprise. "I don't think I like your attitude, dude."

"I don't think I give a rat's ass, *dude*."

"I'm gonna have to ask you to please leave the store, sir."

Dan placed his palms on the counter and leaned in toward the young man. In an angry whisper he said, "Listen, you little shit. You're gonna put a double cheeseburger, medium fries, and a medium Coke on a tray and slide it across this counter to me, or I'm going to rip off your goddamn head and shove it so far up your ass you'll think you're stuck in a chocolate Frosty."

The kid snorted. "Chocolate Frosty. Good one, dude." The kid stood there in thought for a second. "I could call the cops."

"Your head'll be in your ass long before they get here," Dan warned.

"Fine." The young man placed Dan's order. When it was up, he handed Dan his tray. "Here you go, sir," he said. "Here's your Dave's Double *with cheese*."

"Thank you," Dan said.

He grabbed the tray and went to join his friends in the booth. Stopping at the condiment island for ketchup, the old lady accosted him.

"I overheard you speaking so rudely to that young man," she said venomously. "A man your age should know better than to use such profound language in public. It's outrageous, the civil discourse that has become epidemic in our country! Aren't you ashamed?"

Without missing a beat, Dan bent down, cupped his hand over the old crow's ear, and whispered. The color left he face, and it seemed her petite body had turned to stone. Dan left her standing there, mute and immobile.

"Hey, what did you say to that old lady?" Red asked as Dan sat down.

"I made her an indecent proposal."

"And?" Richard inquired.

"I think she's considering it," Dan replied, grinning. "Let's eat quickly and get the hell out of here."

Chapter Fourteen

"Loaded?" Maxine hollered from the kitchen. "How loaded?"

"I don't know," Dan yelled back from the bathroom. He flushed the toilet and lowered the seat. "I didn't ask."

"Are you going to ask him?"

"I don't know." Dan opened the medicine chest in search of the toothpaste. The cabinet seemed to be much fuller than usual. Maxine's creams, serums, lotions, and cleansers had been slowly taking over. They were spreading like triffids after a colorful meteor shower. Dan picked up one of the small glass jars and read the label; SEACRET: MINERALS FROM THE DEAD SEA, it said in gold letters. *I wonder how much this cost.* He thought. He placed the jar back on the shelf and grabbed his toothpaste.

"You almost done in there?" Maxine called out.

Dan ignored the question and kept brushing. *Minerals from the Dead Sea*, he thought. If he could shake his head and brush his teeth at the same time, he would have.

Maxine was standing at the stove frying two T-bone steaks in a large cast iron frying pan when Dan entered the kitchen.

"Why didn't you cook those on the grill?" Dan asked.

"Because that grill is falling apart," Maxine replied. "You need a new one."

"That grill is just fine," Dan argued. "What's with all the Dead Sea shit?" Dan walked back into the dining room to the bar and made himself a tequila and 7UP.

"Dead Sea shit?" Maxine replied.

"All that shit in the medicine chest." Dan returned to the kitchen, a drink in one hand and the morning edition of the *Key West Citizen* in the other.

"A woman I work with is selling it."

"And you couldn't say no."

"Why would I say no? It's really good stuff."

"How much did it cost?"

"It doesn't matter."

"How much was that little jar of face cream?"

"Why do you want to know?" Maxine jabbed one the steaks with a fork and flipped it over.

"I'm just curious."

"You just want to make fun of me."

"I'm not going to make fun of you."

"It was seventy-five dollars."

"Are you shittin' me!"

"See, you're mad."

"I'm not mad. It's your money. You can waste it however you want."

"I'm not wasting it if I'm using it."

"That jar is only 1.7 ounces. That's almost forty-five dollars an ounce."

"It comes from the Dead Sea," Maxine argued.

"My soap comes from the springs of Ireland, and I get eight bars for six bucks."

"Oh, that's very funny," Maxine said angrily.

"Get it?" Dan asked. "Springs of Ireland, because it's Irish Spring."

"Yeah, I got it, smart ass. Get out of the kitchen before I stick this fork in you."

Dan walked toward the back door. He opened the neck of his T-shirt and took a deep sniff. "Ah, Irish Spring! Manly, yes, but I like it too." He laughed at his own joke and said, "I should have been a comedian."

"Stick with smart-ass," said Maxine. "You're really good at that."

Dan walked down the steps and along the gravel path to the two Adirondack chairs that sat next to the fire pit. He took a seat in one of the chairs and took a sip of his drink. He set the drink on the ground next to his chair, and opened the newspaper.

Halfway through the comics, Buddy lumbered up beside Dan's chair, sniffed his knee, and laid down beside him.

"Hey, pal," said Dan. "What's going on?"

Buddy pressed his chin into the grass and closed his eyes.

"No kidding?" said Dan. He went back to the funnies.

Twenty minutes later, Dan was startled awake by Maxine's hollering from the back door. "Hey, are we eating outside?"

"Huh? Yeah."

Maxine disappeared back into the kitchen.

"You need my help?" Dan called out.

"That would be nice."

Dan climbed out of his chair with a groan and went for the back door.

Maxine already had the plates made when Dan got inside. "What do you want me to carry?" Dan asked.

"I'll get the plates," Maxine answered, "you get my wine glass ... and grab the bottle of wine on the dining room table."

"Roger that," said Dan.

Dan sat on one side of the picnic table, and Maxine sat on the other side, the side facing Bev's house. Buddy lay under the table eagerly awaiting any morsel that might hit the ground.

Dan cut into his steak and took a bite. "Perfect," he said.

"See," said Maxine, "I didn't even need the grill."

"Where did that cast iron pan come from?"

"I borrowed it from Bev. We should pick up one next time we're at the store."

"How much does something like that cost?"

"Why?" Maxine joked. "Are you short of cash this week?"

Dan ignored the jab. He had been called cheap before. It didn't bother him then, and it sure as hell didn't bother him now. Dan didn't think of himself as cheap, he thought of himself as more of a bargain hunter. He wouldn't mind buying a new cast iron pan, or even a new grill, for that matter, but finding a perfectly good one on the curbside for free would be awesome.

"Did you hear back from your dad?" asked Maxine.

"Not yet," Dan replied.

"I hope nothing's wrong."

"Nothing's wrong. Mom just forgot to tell him I called, or she told him, and he forgot that she told him. They may have even forgotten they had a son. Either way, they'll blame each other for the mix-up."

"So, you're saying they're forgetful," Maxine said, and chuckled.

"Well, according to her, she's still as sharp as a tack, but he can't remember anything. According to him, he's still sharp as a tack, but she can't remember anything. I think they both just remember to forget the things they remember when it suits them."

"You lost me on that one."

Dan's phone vibrated in his pocket. "Speak of the devil," he said. "Hello?"

"Sonny!" Gene Coast shouted.

"Hey, Dad."

"It's your dad."

"Yeah, I know, Dad. You're the only one who calls me Sonny."

"Your mother says you called last night."

"That was two nights ago," Dan corrected.

"What? She just told me this morning."

"I told you yesterday morning!" Dan heard his mother screech in the background.

"Bull shit!" said Gene. "Woman can't remember shit, Sonny."

"I know, Dad. And you're still sharp as a tack."

"I can remember serial numbers from jet parts I installed in Nam, and she can't remember to put mayonnaise on both pieces of bread when she makes me a sandwich. Over forty years and she can't put mayonnaise on both slices of bread. Woman got a mind like a screen door."

"You don't need all that mayonnaise, ya old fool," Peg shouted. "It's not good for your blood pressure!"

"You know what else ain't good for my blood pressure, woman?" Gene yelled back. "You hollerin' at me constantly."

Dan held the phone away from his ear as his parents continued to bicker at each other. "What the Christ?" he whispered. He put the phone on speaker, laid it on the table, and cut into his steak. He put the piece in his mouth and slowly chewed.

"It's like dinner theater," Maxine commented.

"Yeah," Dan agreed. "Someday we'll probably be listening as it turns into one of those murder mystery dinners."

Maxine giggled.

"Sonny?" Gene said. "Sonny, are ya there?"

Dan picked up his cell. "Right here, Dad."

"Thought I lost ya."

"Am I on speaker, Dad?"

"No. Why?"

"I need to talk to you in private. Can you walk outside for a second?"

"Private? Why, what's the problem?"

"No problem, Dad. Just walk outside for a minute. I have to ask you something."

"I'll walk outside, but your mother will probably follow me right out there."

"That's a risk we'll have to take, Dad." Dan waited as his father walked outside. Maxine continued to grin from across the table. "Knock it off," Dan whispered to her.

"I'm out in the backyard. Go ahead."

"Dad, when you were in Viet—"

"Hold on. Your mother is staring at me through the kitchen window."

"Good God."

"I'm gonna go inside the shed."

"Yeah, Dad, that won't look suspicious at all. You go right on inside that shed."

"Shit, the door is locked. I left my keys inside. I'm gonna have to run back in the—"

"Dad, does the name Tran Pham ring a bell?"

"Amtrak?"

"No, Dad. Tran Pham," Dan repeated a little slower.

"Tran Pham, Tran Pham. Why does that sound familiar?"

"Did you know a young woman in Vietnam named Tran Pham?"

"Oh my God," Gene whispered. "I, uh … I, uh, haven't heard that name in a long long time." Gene's voice

111

cracked a little as he spoke. His voice sounded faraway and nostalgic. "A very long time."

"So you remember her?"

"Of course."

"Dad ... she has a son."

"A son?"

"He's forty-six." Dan paused while his father did the math.

"Oh, my."

Dan had never in his life heard his father utter the words "oh my." He wondered if he had ever said them before, or if maybe those two words had been reserved for this exact occasion.

"Are you okay, Dad?"

"Yeah, Danny, I'm fine."

"Her son's name is Richard Bong. He's here in Key West."

"What does he look like?"

"He looks like a guy who's half Vietnamese and half American."

"Is he good? I mean, is he doing okay?"

"He's doing good, Dad. He wants to meet you."

"Tran told him I was his father?"

"Yes."

"Maybe we should take the train down to your place."

"Why don't you just fly, Dad?"

"Your mother would never fly. We'll take the train to Miami and rent a car from there."

"Okay, Dad."

"I'll explain everything to your mother, and get back to you with the details."

"Sounds good."

"Talk to ya later, Sonny."

"Good luck, Dad."

"You got that right." Gene hung up the phone and Dan placed his on the table.

"Maybe I should have flown up to their place," said Dan.

"I'm sure everything will be fine," Maxine responded. "This all happened before the two of them ever met."

"Yeah, but it's still a lot for them to take in."

Maxine reached out and put her hand on Dan's. "It'll be fine."

Dan glanced down at the diamond on Maxine's finger, and then up at her eyes, which were focused on the ring. "Are you really consoling me, or did you just want to look at that ring again?"

"A little of both, babe. A little of both."

Chapter Fifteen

Friday afternoon Dan dropped Maxine off at work and then headed over to Red's Bar and Grill. He backed into his usual spot and made the trek across the crushed stone parking lot. He pulled open the door and stepped inside. When his eyes adjusted to the darkness, and he could see Red standing behind the bar, he grinned big and said, "There he is."

Red grimaced. "There who is?" he asked.

"There you are," Dan replied, pointing at the big guy as he crossed the sticky wooden floor. "Excited?"

"Excited about what?"

"You know what." Dan took a seat on his favorite orange stool. "The big date."

"It's not a *big* date. It's just a date. We're going to dinner and that's it."

"What do you mean, 'and that's it'? There could be more."

"Stop it."

"You have condoms?"

"Really, just shut up."

"You can't be too careful these days."

"You want a drink?"

"Maxine said I could only have two drinks tonight."

"So that's a yes?"

"Yes."

As he prepared his friend's drink, Red asked, "Are you going to ask Richard about his stores?"

"At some point," Dan replied. "I spoke with my father last night."

"Oh yeah. What did he have to say?" Red slid Dan's drink across the bar to him.

"He said he remembers Richard's mother."

"Does he remember her loving him long time?"

"Wow, that's kinda racist."

"How can it be? It was in a 2 Live Crew song."

"You're an idiot."

"That's been established. Does he remember making love to her?" Red asked. "How was that? Was that better?"

"A little," said Dan. "We didn't get into it that much, but he didn't seem surprised, so I figure he remembers."

"So, it's looking like Richard could really be your brother."

"It's looking that way," Dan admitted. "Where is Richard?"

"I left him at my place. He said he wanted to do some sightseeing."

"Okay," Dan said, "then back to you. Are ya nervous about tonight?"

"Not yet!" Red scolded. "But if ya keep talking about it I will be."

Dan glanced up at the clock behind the bar. It was 3:32. "What time is the date?"

"You can't let it go, can ya?"

"I just asked what time it was, for chrissakes."

"I'm picking her up at seven."

"Where are you going to dinner?"

"I got us a table on the patio at Latitudes. I thought we could have a nice dinner and watch the sunset."

"Woo … romantic."

"Shut up," said Red. "Have you and Maxine ever been there?"

"Never been."

"Have you been anywhere on this island other than this bar?" Red made himself a rum and Coke.

Dan waved his arm around the bar like a spokes-model at a gun show. "Where else could I possibly need to go? This place has everything: shitty food, shitty booze, and a shitty atmosphere."

"Wow, my best friend."

"You know, I told Maxine we were best friends."

"That was stupid," Red shot back. "You're supposed to tell your girlfriend that *she's* your best friend."

"Why would I tell her that?"

"Because that's just what you do."

"But I would be lying."

"So? That's a lie every guy tells. No guy's wife or girlfriend is their best friend. You just say you are. It's like, 'no, those jeans don't make your butt look big.' Those jeans can make her butt look four ax handles wide, but you stick to your story."

"Huh," said Dan. "I knew about the butt thing, but I shit you not, no one ever told me about the best friend thing."

"You learn something new every day."

"I guess I do."

Red downed the remainder of his drink and then stared into the ice tray contemplating another one.

"What's the matter?" Dan asked.

"Should I have another drink?"

"You're asking me? I remember a day when I would have had nine more drinks before a date."

"Yeah, and I remember at least three different times you puked on a woman."

"Those times were not really my fault."

"How the hell were they not your fault?"

"Come on, really? A woman has to recognize the warning signs. If I start arching my back like a cat yakkin' up a fur ball, you gotta take cover."

"I guess you got a point there," Red said shaking his head.

"Besides, times have changed. I haven't puked on anyone in over two years." Dan reached in his pocket and pulled out his cell. "What's Richard's number?"

"Are we calling him Richard or Rich?" Red asked.

"Either. What's his number?"

"You don't know your own brother's number. Shame on you."

"Come on. Give it up."

Red checked his own cell for the number and rattled it off to Dan as Dan entered it into his contacts. "Thanks," said Dan.

"What did you need the number for?"

"Maybe I'll meet up with him later and we'll hit the town."

"Don't get him into any trouble."

"I wouldn't dream of it."

"Hey!" Red said, having an aha moment. "You know where you should take him?"

"Where?"

"You should take him to see The Amazing Gary," said Red, referencing a local psychic whose abilities Dan found highly suspect.

"Why the Christ would I take him to see that nut?"

"How can you call him a nut?"

"Because, he's a nut."

"I think he more than proved himself the last time we were there."

"How did he prove himself?" Dan asked skeptically. "I'm the one who remembered the license plate number."

"Because he hypnotized you," Red pointed out.

"He didn't hypnotize me," Dan argued. "I was awake the whole time."

"Or were you?"

"Yes, I was," Dan responded. "Why should I bring Richard to see him?"

"Maybe The Amazing Gary could read Richard's mind, or maybe he could talk to Richard's mom from beyond the grave. Maybe she could tell you the whole story."

"Or we could just wait till my dad gets here and see what he has to say. After that, we'll get a DNA test done."

"Boring," said Red. "A quick trip to The Amazing Gary could tell us everything we need to know."

"This conversation is telling me everything I need to know about *you*."

Red checked the clock again.

"Butterflies in your tummy?" Dan asked.

"I need another drink," Red replied, and began making himself one.

Dan slid his glass back across the bar. "Yeah, make me one too."

"That makes two drinks for you."

"Hey, that's pretty good, but Koko the gorilla could count to twenty."

"But could he make a drink?"

"Probably, and he would probably even mop the floor."

"I wonder if he's looking for a job?"

"He's dead."

"Are you shittin' me?"

"Died a few years back."

"That's too bad. I was a big fan of Koko's." Red placed his drink on the bar and started preparing one for Dan.

"I wouldn't be surprised to find out that Koko was *your* long-lost brother," said Dan. "The two of you look a lot alike."

Red slid Dan's drink to him. "I'll take that as a compliment," he said. "That Koko was one good-lookin' monkey."

"Ape."

"What?"

"Ape," Dan repeated. "Koko was an ape."

"What's the difference?"

"Monkeys have tails. Apes, like you and Koko, don't have tails."

Dan turned and looked behind him when he heard the door open; it was Cindy, the bartender.

"Just in time," Red said. "Jump back here behind the bar. I gotta head home and get ready for my date."

"Good luck," Cindy said, as she tied her apron around her waist.

Red halted, and turned around. "You're like the third person who wished me luck."

Dan snickered.

"So?" Cindy replied.

"Why does everyone think I need good luck to go on a date?"

"It's just a figure of speech," Cindy said.

"Whatever." Red spun around and headed for the door. "Talk to ya, tomorrow, Dan."

"Good luck, Koko," Dan responded. "And remember, no flinging your own feces on a first date."

Chapter Sixteen

"Hey, Rich, it's Dan."

"Hey, brother," Richard answered. "What's up?"

"Maxine is working tonight, and uh … I was wondering if you wanted to grab a drink, or something to eat, or something."

"Yeah, that would be great."

"Where ya at?"

"I'm walking back to Red's place," Richard said. "Not the bar. I mean his house."

"I figured that. I just left the bar."

"Did Red calm down yet?"

"Calm down?" Dan asked.

"He was pretty nervous about his big date tonight, when he left here."

"Yeah, he still seemed a little nervous. He's probably home now. He left the bar about an hour ago. He said he had to get ready for the date."

Richard chuckled. "That's funny. What time are you picking me up?"

"Ten minutes."

"Okay. What should I wear?"

"Put on your prettiest sundress," Dan replied, and hung up. *What should I wear?* He thought, mocking Richard in his head.

*****

Dan pulled up in front of Red's house about ten minutes later. Richard's Passat was parked in the driveway, and Red's pink Volkswagen Bug was parked on the street. Dan pulled the Porsche in behind the Bug and shut off the engine.

Dan climbed out of the car and walked across the street. "Honey, I'm home!" he shouted as he walked through the front door.

Richard was sitting at Red's kitchen table. He had the chair leaned back on two legs, against the wall. He was smoking a fat, dark Camacho torpedo.

"That smells good," said Dan.

Richard pointed across the room. "There's a whole box of them on the countertop," he said. "Help yourself."

"Nice!" Dan said. He grabbed himself a cigar and used the cutter that was lying next to the box.

Richard reached into his pocket and pulled out a gold-plated cigar lighter. He handed it to Dan.

Dan inspected the lighter. He read the inscription on the side: THE RICH EAT, THE POOR SMOKE. "Nice lighter," he said. "Interesting inscription too. Where'd you get it?"

"Gift from my dad, when I graduated college. I think the inscription's an old Vietnamese proverb."

Dan lit it up and took a few puffs. "Damn, that's good," he remarked. "Say, why are you sitting out here?"

Richard motioned toward the chair across the table from him. "Sit down," he said, "and enjoy the fashion show."

Dan looked confused. "Fashion show?"

"Sit down," Richard whispered.

No sooner had Dan taken his seat than Red strutted into the room.

"How's this?" Red asked. He walked to the middle of the room and slowly twirled.

"Fashion show", Dan whispered, nodding his head.

Red was dressed in tan slacks, a black dress shirt with a skinny white leather tie tucked between the buttons, and a tan sport coat. The clunky earth shoes Red sported suggested he'd been to Goodwill recently.

"You look like Deney Terrio," said Richard.

Red smiled. "Awesome."

"That's not a good thing," Richard said.

"Unless your date is in 1979," said Dan. "And if that's the case, you're late."

"Who's Deney Terrio?" Red asked.

"It doesn't matter," Dan said. "Put something else on."

Red's shoulders dropped as the wind left his sails. He turned and sulked out of the room.

"That was his second outfit," Richard pointed out.

"Third time's the charm," said Dan.

Dan and Richard puffed their cigars and blew smoke into the air. A few minutes later Red returned to the kitchen. He was dressed in light brown cargo shorts and a blue Hawaiian shirt.

"Perfect!" Dan exclaimed. "You've never looked better."

"This is what I wore all day today," Red responded. "I was wearing this when you were at the bar."

"And I thought you looked beautiful then too," said Dan.

"You didn't even notice."

"I did. I swear."

"I don't know," Red said, tugging at the shorts. "I never liked the way these fit." He turned around. "Do they make my ass look big?"

"Yes," said Richard.

"Your ass *is* big," Dan said.

"You guys are no help at all," Red said.

"Just wear what you have on," Dan said. "You look fine."

"Just *fine*?" Red asked. "I'd like to look better than fine."

"I think that ship sailed at least fifteen years ago," said Dan.

Richard chuckled. "You look good, Red."

"Yeah," Dan added. "I wish I was going on a date with you."

"You're engaged," Richard reminded him.

"That's right," said Red with one last slow twirl, "so you'll be getting none of this."

"Come on, Rich," Dan said. "Let's get out of—" His cell phone rang. He looked at the call screen. "Unknown number."

"Answer it!" Red and Richard shouted in unison.

"Hello?"

"Where's Maggie Harrison?" asked a deep menacing voice.

"Who's this?" Dan asked.

"Where is Maggie Harrison?"

"I have no idea. Are you her father?"

"This is Harrison Harrison," said the man.

Dan snickered. "I'm getting an echo," he said.

"Listen, smart ass, you were warned to stay away from my daughter. I like hav—"

"No, you listen," said Dan. "Your goons told us to stay away, and that's exactly what we did. I haven't seen Maggie, or heard from her since yesterday when she left the restaurant."

"If I find out you're lying to me, you will regret it, Mr. Coast."

"I'm sure I will"—Dan aped a receding echo— "Harrison, Harrison, Harrison,"

Click.

127

"Evidently, Maggie has disappeared," Dan said.

"Are we in trouble?" Red asked.

"I hope not," Dan answered.

Richard put his hand on his stomach. "I gotta poop," he said. "My stomach hasn't been right since yesterday. Must be my nerves. I don't know how you guys deal with this shit." He stood and headed toward the bathroom.

"We're used to it," Red said.

"Yeah," Dan agreed. "We get threatened a lot."

"Some people just don't like us," Red added.

"They're just jealous," said Dan.

Red nodded his head in agreement. "Haters gonna hate."

Chapter Seventeen

The following morning at 6:30, Dan kissed Maxine goodbye at the front door. He was shirtless and wearing a pair of blue and white striped boxers.

"Remember," Maxine said, "Colton is starting on the ceiling today."

Dan turned his head and looked over his shoulder at the cannon ball-sized hole. "It's Saturday," he complained. "Who works on Saturday?"

Maxine cocked her head. "Um, I'm working today … on Saturday."

"Yeah, but you're a nurse."

"What's that supposed to mean?"

Dan shrugged. "I don't know," he said. "What time does Colton start work?"

"He said he starts at nine on Saturdays."

"How's your head?"

"Fine. Why?"

"You were pretty drunk when you and Richard picked me up at work last night."

"I only had a couple."

"I bet," Maxine responded. "How did you talk Rich into being your designated driver?"

"I promised him a fantastic home-cooked breakfast this morning."

"You're making him breakfast?"

"I guess I am now."

"You didn't know I was working today, did you?"

"Nope."

"And you thought I would be making the breakfast."

"Yup."

"There's a calendar stuck to the door of the fridge with a magnet," said Maxine. "All you have to do is look."

"Too much trouble. Just tell me when you're working."

"I always do."

"And then I forget."

"That's why I put the calendar up."

"It's a vicious cycle."

Maxine kissed Dan again. "Love ya."

"Back at ya," Dan replied.

Maxine turned and walked down the steps to her car.

Dan shut the door, turned, and looked down at Buddy, who was asleep on his flannel bed next to the small wooden table that held the photograph of Alex, his deceased wife.

"Hey," Dan said.

Buddy opened his eyes and looked up at his master.

"I'll have two eggs over medium, bacon, and white toast," Dan said.

Buddy closed his eyes and his head dropped.

"Really?" Dan asked. "I get your breakfast for you every morning, but I ask you one time to make me an egg, and it's too much trouble? I'll remember that."

He walked into the kitchen to make a pot of coffee.

As the water dripped through the coffee grounds and into the pot, Dan stood with the refrigerator door open. His eyes went from the eggs to the bacon, and back to the eggs. He shut the door and went to the cupboard for a Pop-Tart. Sitting on the top shelf of the cupboard was a box of blueberry Pop-Tarts. Dan grabbed the box; it felt light. He opened the top and looked inside. There was one Pop-Tart inside an open wrapper. He pulled out the breakfast treat and took a bite. It was stale and chewy. *Dammit!*

"What's for breakfast?" Richard asked from the doorway. He, too, was shirtless and wearing yesterday's cargo shorts.

Dan spun around. His eyes focused on Richard's well-defined pecs and six-pack abs.

"We're going out to breakfast," Dan responded. "Looks like you could use a little meat on those bones, Bruce Lee."

"Bruce Lee?" Richard looked down at his chest and stomach. "That's kind of racist," he pointed out.

"Can't be racist," Dan argued. "My brother is Vietnamese."

"I guess you got a point there, but Bruce Lee was Chinese."

"I can't tell the difference."

Richard chuckled. "I know what you mean, round-eye," said Richard. "Whitey all look the same to me."

Dan burst out laughing. Richard had grown on him in the last few days; he couldn't deny that he liked him. And he was really starting to like the idea of having a brother, his own flesh and blood, in his life.

The coffee stopped dripping and Dan turned toward the cupboard. "Coffee?" he asked.

"Sounds good," Richard said.

Dan grabbed two mugs out of the cabinet and poured the coffee. "Cream or sugar?"

"Black."

Dan handed Richard his mug. "I'm gonna slip on some shorts and drink this down by the fire pit."

"Okay."

"Grab the newspaper off the porch and I'll meet you down there."

Richard turned and headed for the porch, and Dan went down the hall to his bedroom.

Dan made a pit stop at the bathroom before going to the bedroom to get his shorts, wadded up on the floor next to the bed, from the day before. He slipped on the shorts and then turned to look at himself in the mirror over the dresser. He sucked in his gut, and pushed it back out. The running he had been doing lately had taken off a few pounds, but his physique looked nothing like his big brother's. *Stupid abs*, Dan thought.

Richard's coffee mug sat on the lawn next to his chair. He held the unfolded newspaper in front of him. When he heard the back door open, his head turned toward Dan. He stared at Dan until he reached him. The look on Richard's face told him something was wrong.

"What's the matter?" Dan asked.

Richard turned the paper so Dan could see the headline: WEST PALM BEACH MAN HANGS HIMSELF IN JAIL CELL.

"Shit," Dan said.

Richard began reading. "Steven Foster, twenty-two, of West Palm Beach, Florida was found hanging in his jail cell at the Palm Beach County Detention Center Friday morning, one week after his arrest for the murder of Adelaide Harrison. Adelaide Harrison was the wife of prominent West Palm Beach attorney Harrison Harrison. Steven Foster was arrested in Haines City, Florida, after a three-day manhunt involving the sheriff's offices of Polk and Palm Beach counties, Haines City Police Department, as well as Florida State Police. Mr. Foster was discovered hiding out in a Haines City motel, along with the girlfriend he had kidnapped, Margaret Harrison the daughter of Harrison and his late wife. West Palm Beach police say that Mr. Foster—"

"That's enough," Dan said. He took a sip of his coffee and sat down in the other chair.

"What are we going to do?" Richard asked.

"I don't know," Dan said.

Richard took a big gulp of his coffee. "I gotta poop."

Chapter Eighteen

After breakfast Dan and Richard jumped back in the Porsche and headed over to Red's Bar and Grill. Dan was talking on his cell phone when they pulled into the parking lot.

"Okay, Dad, I got it," Dan said.

"We'll be getting to your place around seven o'clock Monday evening," said Gene.

"Yeah, that's the third time you told me, Dad." Dan backed into his spot and shut off the engine.

"Did he write it down?" Peg hollered in the background.

"What?" Gene shouted.

"Did he write it down?" Peg screamed.

"Your mother wants to know if you wrote it down."

"No, I didn't write it down."

"Get a pen and write it down. Monday evening around seven."

"What's happening at seven on Monday?" Dan joked.

"That's when we're—"

"I know, Dad. I was joking."

"So then you did write it down?"

"I'm not gonna write it down, Dad."

"What if you forget?"

"So what if I do? I'll remember when you knock on the door."

"The little smart-ass won't write it down, Peg."

"I gotta go, Dad," Dan said. "I'll see you on Wednesday."

"Mond—"

Dan hung up the phone.

"I can't wait to meet them," said Richard.

"Oh, it'll be a treat."

"What are they like?"

"Well, one of them is bat shit crazy. And the other is a little worse." Dan opened his door and got out.

"Who's who?" asked Richard.

"I haven't decided yet. You'll have to make that call on your own."

"I can't wait."

The two men crossed the parking lot and went inside; Red was behind the bar. "Did you see the headline?" he asked when they entered.

"We sure did," Dan replied. "It scared the shit out of Rich."

"Shut up," Richard whispered.

"You shut up," Dan shot back. "It's fun having a brother. I can't wait till our first fight—wait, you don't know karate, do you?" Dan took a seat at his favorite stool Richard sat next to him.

"That's also kind of racist," said Richard.

"No it's not," Dan argued. "Every Asian person I saw on TV when I was growing up knew karate, so asking if you know karate can't be racist."

"Dan, those shows were full of offensive racial stereotypes."

Dan chuckled. "Wow," he said. "You're gonna sit there and tell me that Kung Fu was racist?"

Richard shook his head. "Rum and Coke," he said to Red.

"Kung Fu was part American, just like you, ya know," said Red. "He knew karate."

"That's right," said Dan. "He was part Asian, part American."

"First of all," Richard responded. "He knew kung fu, not karate. And his name wasn't Kung Fu. It was Kwai Chang Caine. The *show* was called Kung Fu. He wasn't Vietnamese, like me. He was Chinese—just like Bruce Lee and karate—and David Carradine, the actor who portrayed him, wasn't Asian at all. He was one million percent Caucasian. Bruce Lee actually developed the concept for the series—a Western with a Chinese hero, but network execs passed on him starring in it, saying he was too Oriental looking. You can't get more racist than that, guys. *Kung Fu* was the one show with Asian characters that I liked because it presented them in a positive light, and some of the folks Caine met in his travels were rightly portrayed as bigots."

"Wow, Rich, you're pretty smart," Red observed. "Are you sure you're Dan's brother?"

Dan laughed. "Yeah, Rich, you've sure got a lot going on upstairs. Not to mention, all this time I thought I was the big TV buff in the family. You sure seem to know a lot about American TV, Rich."

"I grew up in Texas," Richard reminded him. "I watched all the same shows growing up that you did."

"Tequila, Seven, and lime," Dan ordered. He turned back to Richard. "But you realize none of that answered my question."

"What question?" Richard asked.

"Do you know karate?"

"It doesn't matter."

"Do ya?"

"Yes!"

"Ha!" Dan shouted. "You are so racist."

Red pushed Dan's rocks glass across the bar to him. Dan took a big gulp.

"What are we gonna do?" Red asked.

"About what?" Dan asked.

"About Maggie Harrison."

"We're not doing anything," Dan said. "I like being alive."

"I bet Maggie's mom and Steve Foster liked being alive as well," said Richard.

"Not you too," said Dan.

"We can't just sit by while that young girl gets murdered," Richard said.

"Did you ever call Joey Pantucco back?" Red asked.

"Nope," said Dan. "I haven't had time."

"Been too busy doin' nothin', huh?" said Red.

"Tell him the rest," said Richard.

"Rest of what?" Red asked.

"Maggie Harrison's father called this morning," said Richard.

"Called you?" Red asked Dan.

"Of course he called me," Dan said. "Who else would he call?"

"What did he want?"

"He wanted to know if I had seen Maggie."

"Why, did he misplace her?"

"Evidently."

"Does he think we had something to do with it?"

"Probably."

"His henchman are probably already on their way."

"My stomach hurts," said Richard.

"No one is on their way anywhere," said Dan.

"Did you try to call Maggie?" Red asked.

"No," Dan answered.

"Don't you think you should? And then give Joey P a call."

Just then the door burst open and smacked into the wall behind it. Light flooded the room. Dan and Richard spun around. They all three shaded their eyes against the bright sunlight. A tall lanky shadow figure stepped through the door.

"Yo, dudes!" Skip shouted. "Did you see today's headline?"

Chapter Nineteen

Dan and Richard helped Skip to a wooden chair at one of the four-tops near the jukebox. Red poured a glass of water for the young man, and hurried it to the table.

"What the hell are you doing here?" Dan asked. "Why aren't you in the hospital?"

"They ain't built a hospital yet that can hold me," Skip shot back.

"I don't really think hospitals are built to hold anyone," Dan said.

"What about mental hospitals?" Red asked.

"I wish one would hold you," Dan responded.

"Oh, yeah? Well I wish … shut up."

"Good comeback."

Skip looked Richard up and down, sizing up the man. "This my replacement?" he asked.

Richard gave Dan a confused look.

"I'll explain later," Dan said. He returned his attention to Skip. "Were you discharged?"

"I discharged myself, amigo," Skip said.

"How are you feeling?" Red asked, handing Skip the glass of water. "Here, drink this."

"I'm fine," said Skip. "They were gonna let me out in the morning anyway."

"How do you know that?" Dan asked.

"Because the doctor said, 'I'll be in tomorrow morning to see you, and then we'll get you out of here.'"

"Maybe we should give the hospital a call just to make sure," said Richard.

"Oh, you'd like that, wouldn't you?" Skip replied. "Why don't you just mind your own business?"

"I'm just trying to help."

"No one asked ya."

"Calm down, Skip," said Dan. "No one is replacing you." Dan turned to Richard. "Rich, this is our friend Skip—"

"Best friend," Skip interrupted.

"I'm his best friend," Red argued.

"We're all friends!" Dan shouted. "No one is replacing anyone. Skip, this is my … brother, Richard Bong. Rich, this is Skip Stoner."

"Bong," Skip sneered. "What kind of name is that?"

"It's Vietnamese," Richard answered.

"A Vietnamese Dick Bong," said Skip.

"Yeah, yeah," said Richard. "I've heard them all before."

"Dick Bong," Red snickered. "I didn't even think of that."

"Okay then," said Dan. "Now, we're all friends. So you can all stop acting like—"

"Did you see the headline in the newspaper this morning?" Skip shouted.

"Yes, we saw it!" said Dan. "Stop yellin', for chrissakes."

Skip used his inside voice. "What are we gonna do?"

"I'm gonna have another drink," Dan said. He handed his empty glass to Red.

"How many did Maxine say you could have today?" Red asked.

"Just make the damn drink."

"She's rationing you, dude?" Skip asked. "That's really pathetic."

"She was a little angry last night when we picked her up," said Richard. "He was pretty drunk."

"Shut up, Rich," Dan ordered.

"Maxine said he could only have two yesterday," said Red.

"He went way over that," Richard responded.

"Okay, that's enough," said Dan. "You gonna make that drink, or am I gonna head over to the Green Parrot?"

Red turned without answering and headed for the bar.

"That's what I thought," said Dan.

"I'll ask again," said Skip. "What are we gonna do about this?"

"Tell him the rest," said Richard.

"Will you stop doing that?" Dan bitched.

"Maggie's father called this morning to see if we had heard from her," Richard explained.

"Yo, dude, are you saying he doesn't know where she is?"

"Sounds that way," said Dan.

"I think he already killed her," Red called out from the bar, "and he only called to give himself an alibi."

Dan looked back over his shoulder at Red, partly because he was wondering when his drink was coming, but also because he thought Red might have made a good point.

"I think you better call her," Richard prodded.

"Maybe you're right," Dan said. He took out his cell phone and scrolled through his contacts. When he got to Maggie's name, he hit the call icon.

We're sorry, you have reached a number that has been disconnected or is no longer in serv—

Dan hung up. "Still not in service," he said.

"How did she call you the other day?" Skip asked.

"I don't know," Dan replied. "She called me from an unknown number."

"Hmm, interesting," Skip mused, then abruptly switched gears. "How was your trip up to West Palm?"

"Don't ask," said Richard.

"Too late, bro. Already did."

"Maggie's father sicced his goons on us," Dan said.

"He has goons?" asked Skip.

"Several," Richard said.

"I hate goons," said Skip.

"Me too."

Skip asked, "What did the goons have to say?"

"They threatened us," Richard replied, "and told Dan if he ever called her or spoke to Maggie again, they would kill all of us."

"Like they did Steve Foster," Red interjected. He placed Dan's drink on the table in front of him.

"Two down, one to go," said Richard.

"What's that mean?" Skip asked.

"That's what Maggie over heard her father say," Red answered. "She even recorded it on her phone."

"And she thinks she's the third," Skip surmised.

"Yut," said Dan. "And it's starting to look like she might have been right."

"What are we gonna do about it?" asked Skip.

"First, we're gonna get you back to the hospital," Dan replied.

"Aw, come on, dude," Skip complained. "Why ya gotta harsh my gig like that?"

"Harshing gigs is my middle name," Dan responded.

"You gonna call Joey P?" Red asked.

"I'll call him after I get Skip back to the hospital."

"Bogus!" said Skip. "Truly bogus."

Chapter Twenty

Skip was pretty angry when Dan and Richard left him at the emergency room and told the doctor on call that he had escaped. They said a quick goodbye and told Skip they would see him tomorrow—that is, if the doctor sprung him.

On their way back to Red's, Dan took out his cell phone and dialed Joey Pantucco's number.

"It's about time you called me back, ya crazy bastard," Joey answered. "The word on the street is that you went and got yourself in trouble again." Even though Joey Pantucco had moved to Miami with his family when he was just a kid, he still had the wise guy, mobster accent, and sounded like he was straight off the set of *The Sopranos*.

"I've been busy, Joey," said Dan.

Dan and Joey had been friends for a couple of years, ever since Joey mistook Dan for a friend of his missing brother, Jimmy. The truth was, Jimmy Pantucco wasn't missing. Dan had actually killed Jimmy a few months before he met Joey. Only Dan and Red knew the truth, so Dan's secret was safe—if big-mouthed Red didn't spill the beans. As long as Joey never found out, Dan would have a good friend in the Miami underworld.

"Busy doin' what?" asked Joey. "Bein' a friggin' beach bum?"

"When you're good at something, stick with it, I always say."

Joey laughed; he always laughed at Dan. "So tell me, Coast, how the hell did you get mixed up with Harrison Harrison, attorney to the rich and scumbags?"

"It was an accident, Joey."

"It always is with you, Coast."

"Red and I met his daughter, Maggie, and her boyfriend, Steve Foster, at a hotel in Haines City. Evidently, she was running from her father. She had a few bruises and a fat lip. Her and the boyfriend said Harrison had done it to her."

"Sounds like Harrison."

"Early the next morning, the cops raided the place and arrested the boyfriend. One of the cops at the scene told me that Foster had killed Harrison's wife. Three days later, I get a call from Maggie asking me to meet her at a restaurant in West Palm Beach. She tells me it was her father who killed her mother. She says her boyfriend was set up."

"The boyfriend they found hanging in his cell yesterday?"

"You heard?"

"Of course I heard," said Joey. "I've been following this whole to do since I found out you was involved."

"I'm not involved, Joey," Dan argued. "I don't want anything to do with this. Harrison's goons grabbed us outside the restaurant in West Palm after we met with Maggie. They had a message from Harrison: never contact Maggie again, or we would all be dead. I believe him."

"You *should* believe him."

"Is there anything you can do to get him off my back, Joey?"

"Sure, Coast. I'll just give him a call and tell him you're one top-notch guy, and to leave you alone."

"Can you do that?"

"Fuck no, I can't do that," Joey shot back. "You're on your own on this one. I got a lot of friends, Coast, but not many who want to get on Harrison's bad side."

"Why is everyone so scared of this guy?"

"It's not him people are scared of. It's the people he represents. He's got a client list from New York to Bolivia. And they all love him for the acquittals he's gotten them. His clients' got mayors, judges, and cops in their pockets. Probably even meter maids. Harrison is pretty much untouchable because of his relationships with these people."

"So what do I do?"

"Whatever he tells you to do."

"That's what I've done so far, but it doesn't seem to help. I got a call from him this morning. Maggie has disappeared, and I'm afraid he thinks I might have something to do with it."

"Do you?"

"Christ no, Joey. I'm a coward, you know that."

"Yeah, you are kind of a pussy, Coast."

"Exactly … ouch. I told Maggie to go to the cops."

"That was probably a big mistake. She could be missing because she's already dead. Harrison may have called just to throw you off his scent."

"That's what Red said."

"How is that big palooka?"

"Red? He's good."

"Youse guys gotta get back up here and have a meal with me. Nothin' I love more than watching that Sasquatch eat pasta."

"Yeah, if we live through this."

"If that kid's already dead, you probably have nothing to worry about."

"That doesn't make me feel any better, Joey."

"Well, it's all I can give you. Like I said, I can't help you on this one, but I'll call you and let you know if I hear anything."

"Anything like what?"

"Like if he puts a hit out on you, or somethin'."

"Gee, thanks, Joey."

"No problem. I have to hang up. I gotta thing in ten minutes. You take care of yourself, Dan."

"Why did you just call me Dan?" Dan asked suspiciously.

"It's your name."

"But you usually call me Coast. You said Dan like you might never see me again."

Joey burst out laughing. "Hey, ya never know." The call ended.

"Now *I* gotta poop," said Dan.

"Guess it runs in the family," Richard replied.

Dan shuddered. "Did ya have to say runs? My butthole's already puckering like a duck-faced teen on Instagram."

Dan turned into Red's parking lot and backed into his spot.

"Did ya call Joey P?" Red asked, the second Dan and Richard walked back through the door.

"Of course," Dan replied. "I called him on the way here."

"Thank God," said Red. "Is Joey gonna throw a little scare into Harrison to get him off our backs?"

"Nope," said Richard. "It's worse."

"Joey's gonna *kill* Harrison?" Red conjectured.

"Worse," Dan said.

Red cocked an eyebrow. "What's worse than killing someone?" Red asked.

"Not doing anything at all," Richard answered.

"What do you mean?"

"Joey said he can't help us on this one," Dan explained.

"Not at all?"

"Well, he did say he would give us a heads-up when Harrison's guys were on their way down here to murder us."

"That's a big help," Red said with some sarcasm.

"At least we'll know it's coming," said Richard.

"I'm sure everything is gonna be fine," said Dan. "We did everything Harrison told us to do … or told us not to do, I guess."

"Nothing from Maggie?" Red asked.

"Nope," Dan replied. "And I tried her cell a few times. The service is still off."

"I wonder where she is?" Richard pondered.

"I can't imagine," Dan answered. "I just hope she's still alive. Poor kid. We should have done something."

"Little late now, pal," said Red.

"Tequila, Seven, and lime," said Dan. "Maybe that'll make me feel better."

Chapter Twenty-One

The remainder of Saturday was uneventful. Richard moved his luggage to Dan's house and the two men hung around the beach and backyard, having a few drinks and getting better acquainted. Dan introduced Richard to his neighbors: Bev, Mrs. McGee, and old man Stein. Edna McGee asked Richard what his favorite kind of cookie was. He told her it was peanut butter. Dan told Richard to expect a couple dozen within a day or two. Both men were passed out in the two Adirondack chairs by eleven o'clock, when Maxine arrived home, after working a double shift.

Sunday was Maxine's day off. She spent most of it cleaning up Dan and Richard's mess from the day before. "Just what I always wanted to do," she commented at one point. "Clean up after two grown men."

"See," Dan told her, "dreams do come true."

Around noon on Sunday, Dan got a call from Skip; he was cleared to check out of the hospital. Dan and Richard jumped into Richard's Passat, and headed to the hospital to pick him up.

"Dude, can we stop by the pharmacy?" Skip asked. "The doc phoned in a couple prescriptions for me."

"Sure," Richard said. "How do I get there?"

"The CVS on Truman Avenue," Skip replied. "Take a right up here."

"How come you go to CVS?" Richard inquired.

Skip shrugged. "I don't know, dude," he replied. "It's just where I've always gone."

"You should try a locally owned pharmacy," Richard suggested.

Skip nodded. "That's right, bro, you own a bunch of drug stores, don't ya?"

Richard looked over at Dan with an uncomfortable grin. "Well, not a bunch."

Dan hadn't told Richard he knew about all seven pharmacies. He didn't want Richard to know that he had had Rick Carver run a check on him. Now he wouldn't have to; it would look like Skip spilled the beans.

"A *bunch* of drug stores?" Dan asked, feigning ignorance. "I thought you said you only had one pharmacy."

"Well," Richard allowed, "I have a few."

"Seven," Skip said.

"How would you know that?" asked Richard.

"Yeah," Dan jumped in. "How would you know that, Skip? What did you do, have my brother checked out?" This was working out perfectly.

"Yeah, Skip," said Richard. "Fill us in. I'm all ears."

"I called my dad in Jacksonville—he's a cop Rich—and had him run a background check," Skip said. "You can't be too careful these days, dudes."

"What else did you find out?" Richard prodded.

"Well … the reports indicate you're a pretty good guy," Skip stated.

"Thanks," Richard said.

"Don't mention it, dude."

"You're not mad that I checked up on him, are ya, Dan the Man?" Skip asked.

"I guess not," Dan responded.

Richard steered his car into the CVS parking lot and parked in front of Subway.

"Maybe I'll get a submarine sandwich too," said Skip.

"I thought we'd go to Red's for a drink," Dan said.

"That sounds good," Skip returned. "But I want a sub."

Skip got out of the car and disappeared into CVS.

"Can you believe that?" Dan said, shaking his head. "He ran a background check on you."

"Oh that's okay," Richard replied. "I kind of thought you would have."

"Don't be ridiculous," Dan answered, a little nervously. "So, why didn't you tell me you owned so many stores?"

"I don't know. My girlfriend told me not to divulge too much information about myself until we knew for sure if we were brothers."

"So there is a girlfriend."

"Yes."

"She Vietnamese too?"

"No, why?"

"Just wondered," said Dan. "You didn't want me to know you had money just in case we ended up not being brothers."

"Something like that."

"But you knew I had won the lottery, and that I had money."

"Right, but I didn't know how much. For all I knew you had won a couple hundred thousand and had already blown through it."

Dan chuckled. "Good point."

"How much?"

"How much, what?"

"How much did you win?"

"Let's keep that a secret until after the DNA test."

Richard smiled. "You got it."

Skip exited the drugstore carrying two paper prescription bags. He walked down the sidewalk and entered Subway.

"Hot one today," said Richard, trying to make small talk.

"Supposed to be hot all week," Dan replied.

"You think we're going to hear from that Harrison guy again?"

"I think every day that we don't hear from him gives us a better chance of never hearing from him."

"You think Maggie is dead?"

"I try not to think about it."

"I can't stop thinking about it."

"I tried her cell number again this morning. Still nothing."

Skip walked out of Subway grinning. He held his clear Subway bag in the air. Dan nodded his head.

Skip climbed back into the back seat. "I got five chocolate chip cookies too. One for each of us."

"One for each of us?" Dan asked.

You, Rich, Red, me, and … and, uh—isn't there someone else?"

"Like who?" Dan asked.

"Isn't there another guy?"

"Are you sure you're okay?"

"The doc said I might be a little forgetful for a while, but it would get better over time."

"What pills did they prescribe for you?" Richard asked.

Skip placed his food bag on the seat next to him and removed the two pill bottles from their paper bags. "This one's called Carbatrol. I'm only supposed to take it for a week."

"Carbatrol is an anticonvulsant usually prescribed to prevent the severity of convulsions, especially epileptic seizures," Richard observed clinically. "Did you have a seizure?"

"They said I had a couple in the hospital in Bonifay."

"The doctor probably prescribed it to make sure you don't have anymore. What's the other one?"

Skip read the label. "Naproxen."

"That's an NSAID for headaches and other aches and pains," said Richard. "Are you still having headaches?"

"Not really," Skip replied. "They've gotten less frequent."

"Yap, yap, yap," Dan said. "Just give me a friggin cookie."

"They're for when we get to Red's," Skip said.

"I want mine now," Dan complained.

"One more word out of you, mister, and you won't get one at all."

Richard chuckled as he started the car. "You guys are something else."

"Never said we weren't," Dan and Skip said in unison.

"Whoa, dudes, that's freaky," Richard deadpanned.

Chapter Twenty-Two

Gene and Peg Coast pulled into Dan's driveway around five o'clock Monday evening; they were about two hours early. Dan leaned back in his Adirondack chair when he heard the car pull in, and looked up the driveway. He waved when he saw his father climb out of the gray 2018 Toyota Camry they had rented in Miami.

"Sonny!" Gene called out.

Dan turned and looked back across the fire pit at Richard. "It's show time," he said. "How's your tummy, Richie?"

"Shut up, dick head," Richard shot back.

Gene walked down the crushed stone driveway, and then down the gravel path that led to the fire pit. Dan and Richard stood. They were each holding a drink in their hand.

Gene pointed at the drinks. "Hey, you guys do look a little alike." Gene chuckled after his joke. Gene always laughed at his own jokes.

"Dad," said Dan, "This is Richard Bong. Richard … Dad."

Richard held out his hand. "It's a pleasure to meet you, sir," he said. "I've been looking forward to this."

The two men shook hands. Gene stared into Richard's eyes, hoping to see a glimpse of his own past. Hoping to see something that would take him back to a time long ago in a land far away.

"It's great to meet you too, Richard," said Gene.

Dan glanced up the path. "Where's Mom?" he asked.

"I killed her," said Gene.

Dan laughed. "That never gets old, Dad. Now where is she?"

Gene turned around and look behind him. "I don't know. She must have went in the front door."

"Can I make you a drink, Dad?" Dan asked.

"Damn right you can," Gene replied.

Dan walked toward the house and put his hand on Gene's shoulder on his way by. Gene put his hand on top of Dan's. "Nice to see ya, Sonny."

"You too, Dad."

Dan started up the path to the back door. Gene took a seat in Dan's chair. "Well, Richard," he said, "tell me a lot about yourself."

"Okay," said Richard, as he sat back down.

Dan pulled open the screen door and went inside. Maxine and Peg were in the living room. Maxine was showing her the new window. As Dan walked up behind them, they turned, and Maxine pointed up at the ceiling, where the hole used to be. Colton had patched the hole with a new piece of sheetrock and applied three coats of joint compound.

"Is he going to paint it?" Peg asked.

"He's supposed to come back in a couple days and paint it," Maxine replied.

"He's doing a great job."

"I think so," Maxine agreed. "And it would have taken Dan forever to do it."

"He lost his ambition the day John Crow announced those Mega Millions numbers."

"Hey, Mom," Dan said.

Peg went to her son and gave him a hug and a kiss on the cheek. "How are you doing, Danny?"

"Good, Mom."

"You smell like booze."

"That's because I was drinking booze, Mom."

Peg looked at Maxine. "How's he doing with his drinking?" she asked.

"He's going to AA meetings on Monday's and Wednesday's," Maxine replied.

"You went to a meeting this morning?"

"Yes, Mommy," said Dan.

"But you're still drinking?"

"Yes, Mommy."

"So then the meetings aren't helping?"

"This conversation isn't helping," said Dan. He turned and walked over to the bar. "See, now I need a drink."

Peg shook her head. "You're an ass," she said. "I don't know how you put up with him, Maxine. He's just like his father. Got a smart ass comeback for—what is that on your finger?"

Maxine held up her hand, she had a huge smile on her face. "We're engaged!"

Peg threw her arms around Maxine. "Oh my goodness!" she shouted.

"Oh yeah, that's right," Dan said over his shoulder. "I forgot to tell you, Mom, we're engaged."

Peg released her grip. Tears were streaming down her face as she inspected the ring. "It's beautiful."

"Thank you," Maxine responded.

"It ought a be," Dan grumbled. He finished making his and Gene's drinks and started for the back door. "Mom, are you coming out to meet Richard?"

"I want to give the three of you some time alone for a little bit," Peg answered softly.

"You got it," Dan said, and went out the back door. He walked down the path to the fire pit. "How's everything going?"

"Good," Gene replied. "I have so many questions for Richard."

"Just don't ask him if he knows karate," said Dan. "Evidently that's racist."

"It can't be racist," Gene shot back. "I have a Vietnamese son."

Richard chuckled. "Wow, you two are just alike."

"That's what they say," said Dan. He handed Gene his drink and then went to the woodshed to grab another lawn chair. He unfolded it and placed it next to the fire pit between Gene and Richard. "Did you tell Dad you're loaded?"

"No," said Richard. "I didn't mention that."

"He said he's a pharmacist," Gene said.

"He owns several pharmacies in Texas," said Dan.

"Seven," said Richard. "Just seven."

"Wow," Gene said. "Two wealthy sons. I must have done something right." He took a sip of his tequila.

Dan laughed. "Yeah, Dad, you must have."

"Well, Rich, Dan paid off our mortgage and bought us a car when he became wealthy, so I'd say you have some catching up to do."

Richard chuckled. "I guess I do, Gene."

"I'm just bustin' your ovaries, Rich."

"Okay," Dan interrupted, "now that we're all here, Maxine made an appointment for the three of us to get our blood drawn tomorrow for a DNA test. We have to be to Doc Briddle's office first thing tomorrow morning."

"Sounds good," said Richard.

"How long before we get the results?" Gene asked.

"About three or four days," said Dan.

"Wow. That long?"

Dan sipped is drink. "I don't know exactly how much Rich's mother told him, Dad, but can you tell us how this happened?"

"Well, Sonny, when a man and woman have feelings for each other—"

Richard burst out laughing. "Good one, Gene."

Gene jokingly checked his zipper. "Oh," he said, "you mean the joke was a good one. I thought my fly was down." He chuckled.

Dan rolled his eyes "Okay, Dad, enough with the comedy skit. Just tell us how you met."

Gene looked to Richard. "How much did Tran tell you?" he asked.

"Not much," Richard replied. "She was already very sick when she told me about you. She said you were a jet mechanic, and that you were stationed at Da Nang Air Base. She said the two of you dated, and that she didn't find out she was pregnant until after you left."

Gene shrugged. "That's pretty much it," he said. "I had known your mom for about a year before we started dating—she worked on the base. We didn't start seeing each other until about two weeks before I got shipped out. I wrote to her two or three times after I got back to the States. I don't know if she received the first two letters, but the third letter came back." Gene stared into his glass. "Sorry. I never knew."

"It's not your fault," Richard said. "I guess my mother and father just figured it would be better for everyone to just keep it a secret."

"Who did your mother marry?" asked Gene.

"His name was Kim Bong. According to my mother, he was a friend of her brother's. He knew my mother was pregnant when he married her, but agreed to marry her anyway in exchange for a small piece of land. Kim gave the land to his father two years later, before we escaped Vietnam."

"You've lived in the States since you were about two?" Gene surmised.

"Yes."

"All this time," Gene mumbled.

The back door creaked open. The three men turned their heads and watched as Maxine and Peg walked down the steps and made their way to the fire pit.

Dan and Richard once again stood. Dan introduced his mother to Richard. Peg still had a little tear in her eye. Dan wondered if it was a left over from seeing the engagement ring, or a new one caused by meeting Richard.

Richard held out his hand, but Peg went in for the hug instead. The moisture in Richard's eyes said that it had been too long since a mother had hugged him. He hesitantly put his arms around Peg and squeezed.

When the two separated, Peg looked him up and down and said, "You don't look a lot like the rest of my kids." She smiled. "But there's something very familiar in those eyes."

Richard smiled back. "Thank you, Peg."

"DNA test tomorrow," Dan told his mother.

Peg was still looking into Richard's eyes. "I think I already know how that's going to turn out."

Chapter Twenty-Three

Dan, Gene, and Richard sat in the waiting room in Dr. Linda Briddle's office. Gene was flipping through a six-month-old copy of Field & Stream, mostly just looking at the pictures.

"I'm nervous," said Richard.

"Gotta poop?" Dan asked.

Gene glanced over the top of his magazine at Dan.

"Not that kind of nervous," Richard said.

"What kind?"

"What if the DNA doesn't come back a match?"

"Then you still made a few new friends, Rich."

"Thanks, Dan."

"You two aren't gonna kiss, are ya?" Gene asked.

"We just might, Dad," Dan joked.

Richard reached into his pocket for his cell phone. "Crap," he said.

"What is it?" Dan asked.

"I forgot my cell phone in the car. I'll be right back." He got up and went for the door.

Gene watched Richard as he crossed the floor, and as soon as the door shut behind him, he got up and moved to the seat next to Dan. "Hey," he whispered.

"What?" Dan whispered back.

"There's something I didn't tell you."

"What is it?"

"Richard's mother was dating a friend of mine—that's how I knew her. He was my best friend over there. When he went back to the States, her and I still talked. We went to the movies a few times, had a few drinks together, and then the night before I shipped out, we slept together. It was only once."

"So you're saying there's a chance that Rich could be your friend's son?" said Dan.

"Exactly," Gene said. "Here's the thing, Sonny, my buddy's name was Richard Chase."

"Crap," Dan whispered. "But why would Rich's mom tell him that you were his father?"

"Let's just say, out of the two of us—Chase and me—I was the nicer person. He was a big drinker and kind of a prick to her when he was drunk."

"Physically?"

"I saw him smack her a couple times."

"Dammit."

"It might not mean anything. Tran really loved Chase, even if he was a prick. Maybe she just named Richard after Chase because she *wished* he was the father."

"You know where this Richard Chase is now?"

"He was killed in a car accident less than a year after returning home from Vietnam."

The door opened and Richard walked back in. He saw the somber looks on Dan and his father's face. "What's the matter," Richard said, "someone die?"

"Yeah, me," said Gene. "Of old age. How long we gotta sit here?"

Dan glanced up at the clock. "Shouldn't be too much longer."

"That's what you said twenty minutes ago."

"Mr. Coast?" said the receptionist.

Dan and his father both looked over. "Yeah?" they both said.

The receptionist—who gave the impression of someone who had just sucked the juice out of a lemon—looked down at her appointment book. "Dan Coast," she clarified.

"That's me," Dan stated. He got up and walked toward the door to the examining room. Before he got to the door it opened. Doc Briddle stood in the doorway.

"Sorry to keep you gentlemen waiting so long," said Briddle. "I had—oh, who am I kidding? I don't care how long you waited. I get paid the same either way." She didn't crack a smile. Doc Briddle never smiled when delivering her own special brand of dry humor. "Get your ass in here, Coast, and maybe I'll even check your prostate just for fun."

"Not without buying me dinner first, Doc," Dan shot back.

Linda Briddle had been Dan's doctor since he first arrived in Key West. Due to a drunken hammock accident, she put four stitches in the back of his head on his third day on the island.

Briddle was just under six feet tall and outweighed Dan by at least thirty pounds. She had a deep voice and hairier arms than most men Dan knew. On most morning appointments, she had a smooth hairless face, but by the afternoon she sported a five o'clock shadow that would make Fred Flintstone envious. Having been born in Key West, Briddle was a true Conch, as lifelong residents call themselves. Other than her time at Boston University, she had spent her entire life there.

Dan walked through the door and Dr. Briddle started to close it. She paused, and turned back to Gene and Richard. "Why don't you guys come in too," she said, waving them in. "We'll get all y'all at once."

Gene and Richard got up and followed Dan through the door.

"Have a seat, gentlemen," said Briddle, closing the door behind her. "I hear we're drawing a little blood today."

"We're not," said Dan. "You are."

"I *am* the expert," said Briddle. She reached for a box of extra-large rubber gloves that sat on a shelf above a red, wall mounted medical waste container. She slipped her Chewbacca-like hands into the gloves. "Looking for our baby daddy, are we?"

Gene chuckled.

"Oh, yeah, sorry, Doc," Dan said. "Rich, this is Linda Briddle. Doc, Richard Bong; he may be my brother."

"I guess so," Briddle replied. "You look like identical twins, for chrissakes."

Gene burst out laughing even harder.

"Thanks folks," said Briddle. "I'll be here all week."

The three men sat patiently with their arms out and their sleeves rolled up as Briddle gathered the syringes, vials, and other items necessary to take blood samples.

Briddle sat down on a round metal stool with wheels. "Who's up first?"

"I'll go first," said Richard.

Briddle rolled herself over next to Richard. "Now when I get these results back, do I call one of you, or should I just send them over to Maury Povich?"

Chapter Twenty-Four

"That Doc Briddle is a real piece of work," Gene said as he walked up Dan's front steps and onto the porch.

"Yeah," Dan agreed, "she sure is. She's one of the first people I met here."

"Where'd you meet her, at Red's?"

"No, the emergency room."

"What happened?" Richard asked.

"I was drunk, and fell out of my hammock."

"That sounds like something you would do," said Gene. He opened the front door and stepped inside. "Well hello there."

Dan looked past his father to see whom he was talking to. Seated on the couch was Maggie Harrison.

"Oh crap," said Richard.

"Hi guys," said Maggie.

Dan looked around the room. His mother and Maxine were nowhere in sight. "What are you doing here?" he asked.

"I had nowhere else to go," Maggie replied.

"Who is this young lady?" Gene asked.

Maggie stood. "I'm Maggie Harrison. I'm a client of Mr. Coast's."

"No she's not," Dan said. "She's not my client."

"I can pay you," Maggie informed him.

"I don't want your money, Maggie."

"Where's my wife?" Gene asked.

Maggie shrugged. "I don't know. When I got here, I knocked but no one answered. I tried the doorknob and it was unlocked, so I came in and sat down on the couch. You guys came in a few minutes later."

"Swell," Dan said. "They're probably over to Bev's."

"How did you find us?" Richard asked.

Gene walked over to the young woman and held out his hand. "I'm Gene Coast, Dan's father."

"It's nice to meet you."

"How did you find us?" Richard asked again.

"Probably the same way *you* found me," Dan answered.

"Damn Google," Richard said.

"Does your father know you're here?" Dan asked.

"Are you thirsty?" Gene asked. "Would you like a drink?"

"Dad," Dan scolded.

"I'm just being polite to our guest."

"She's not our guest."

"Your client, then."

"She's not my client either. I already told you that."

"*I* need a drink," Richard threw in. He walked straight to the bar.

"Fix me one too," Dan said. He returned his attention to Maggie. "Does your father know you're here?"

"He probably assumes as much."

"Did you go to the cops?"

"Yes."

"What did they say?"

"They told me to go home like a good little girl, and then they phoned my father and told him everything I said."

"Holy crap," Richard said. He spun around. He was pouring straight Scotch in a rocks glass. "What did your father say?" He filled the glass halfway and took a big gulp. It was obvious drinking straight booze was something he didn't do often. It took his breath away, and he struggled to regain his composure. "Is he coming here?" he gasped. He choked and coughed a couple times.

"Slow down with that Scotch," Gene warned.

Richard nodded his head.

"Does he know about the recording on your phone?" Dan asked.

"Yes," said Maggie. "I was thinking we could use it against him."

"How?" Dan asked.

"Like in the movies. We could put it in a safe deposit box, and give the bank manager instructions to release it to the press in the event of any of our deaths. That would keep us all safe."

"Good idea," said Gene.

"No it's not," Dan argued. "This isn't a movie."

Richard was still leaning with his back against the bar. He held his empty glass in his hand. His eyes were a little glassy. "She's right," he said. "It does always work in the movies."

"A recording on a phone isn't enough to scare him," said Dan. "He doesn't even admit to doing anything on that recording."

"Circumstantial evidence," said Gene.

Dan looked at his father. "Been going to law school, Dad?" he asked.

"Nope. Been watchin' a lot of *Law & Order* on the Netflix."

"Anyway, we would need a lot more than that recording to get him to back off," said Dan.

Maggie leaned back on the couch and stuck her hand in the front pocket of her white denim shorts. She pulled out a computer thumb drive and held it up for everyone to see. "Something like this?" she asked.

"What the Christ is that?" Dan asked.

"It's a bunch of files from the computer in my father's office at home."

"What kind of files?"

Maggie shrugged. "I don't know. I didn't have time to look through them. I just downloaded as much as I could before he got home Friday night."

"Give me that," Dan ordered.

Maggie tossed him the thumb drive. Dan tossed it to Richard.

"What do you want me to do with this?" Richard asked.

"Maxine's laptop is on the dresser in our room. Stick that thumb drive in it and see what's on there."

"I don't want to know what's on here," Richard said.

"Well I do."

Richard shook his head and let out a loud sigh. "Fine," he said, and went down the hall.

Dan's cell phone rang. He reached in his pocket and pulled it out. "Unknown number," he read.

"Answer it!" Richard shouted from the bedroom.

"Hello?" said Dan.

"Let me speak to my daughter," said Harrison Harrison.

"Who is this?" Dan asked, knowing full well who it was.

"Let me speak to her right now, smart-ass, and maybe you'll live through this."

"She's not here, Harrison. I told you I haven't spoken with her since your gorillas warned us off."

"I don't believe you."

"You need to trust people more, Harry," said Dan. "Maybe that's something you should bring up to your therapist."

"You talk like a man with a death wish."

"I can't help it," Dan remarked. "She says you killed her mother and her boyfriend, and now you want her dead."

"You know how kids are," was Harrison's response. "They have great imaginations. Did my daughter tell you that the gun that killed her mother was registered to Steven Foster, and that his fingerprints were all over it? Did she tell you that Steve Foster had a violent past? Two young girls that he previously dated, both had restraining orders against him. Did Maggie even bother to tell you that she suffers from schizophrenia and paranoia, and has been on medication to treat those disorders since she was a child? Mr. Coast, you may not approve of the way I make a living, or who I represent, but I haven't killed anyone … yet."

"I heard the recording on her cell phone."

"So did the police, Coast. They didn't think it was anything to be alarmed about."

"You mean the cops in your pocket?"

Harrison chuckled. "You watch too much television, Coast. That, or you have an imagination just like Maggie's. Either way, if my Maggie isn't back in this house by tomorrow afternoon, I'll be sending the gorillas." The call ended.

"What's on that thumb drive?" Dan shouted.

"Still reading!" Richard hollered back.

"Read faster, please!" Dan looked over at Gene. "Dad, I'm bringing Maggie over to Maxine's house. Her old roommate still lives there. It'll be a good place for her to hold up."

"I want to stay here," Maggie said.

"You can't," Dan told her. "I'm sure your father knows where I live by now. You'll be safer at Maxine's place."

Maggie got up. "You're probably right," she said. "I don't want to put any of you in danger."

"Really?" Dan asked. "Don't you think it's a little late for that?"

"Sorry."

"What do you want me to tell your mother and Maxine when they get back?" Gene asked.

"Don't mention anything about Maggie. Just tell them I ran to the liquor store. They'll believe that."

Dan and Maggie walked out the door and to Dan's car. "Thanks for everything you're doing," she said, as they drove down the street.

"Didn't really have a choice, did I?"

"I guess not, but I had no one else to turn to."

Dan took a left onto Bertha Street. "Maggie, your father said that you suffer from schizophrenia and paranoia. Is that true?"

"He left out depression, but yes, it's true."

"Swell."

"Mr. Coast, when I'm on medication, I have no symptoms from my illnesses. My head is perfectly clear. You have to believe me. I may be crazy, but I'm not stupid."

Dan looked over and smiled at the young girl. "Believe it or not, Maggie, this ain't my first wacko rodeo."

Chapter Twenty-Five

Dan returned home about an hour later. He walked through the door carrying two black plastic liquor store bags. In one bag was a bottle of tequila, and in the other, a bottle of Scotch and a bottle of rum.

Richard was sitting on the couch, and Gene was in the recliner with the foot rest up. Both men were idly watching an episode of *Bonanza* on MeTV.

"Can I talk to you for a second?" Richard asked.

Dan put up his index finger. "One second," he answered.

"Where have you been?" Peg asked. She was just walking out of the kitchen and into the dining room.

"I told you he went to the liquor store," Gene said.

"Thought I better stock up," said Dan. He carried the bags to the bar and placed the bottles on top. He crumpled up the bags, went to the kitchen, and tossed them in the garbage. "What's for dinner?"

Maxine was putting away a few of the groceries that Peg had purchased. "Your mother bought a bunch of stuff."

"Stuff like what?" Dan asked.

"Lunch meat, water, the coffee they like, paper towels—"

"We were out of paper towels?"

"No, but she doesn't like the kind we use. Evidently they fall apart when they get wet."

"So what?"

"She likes to dry them and use them a couple times."

Dan smiled. "Yeah, when I was a kid there were always paper towels drying on the back of kitchen chairs. She also used to wash out sandwich bags and use them a few times."

"Frugal," Maxine commented.

"Is that a medical term for insane?"

Maxine slapped Dan on the shoulder. "Be nice."

"I don't know how."

"Where did you go?"

"Liquor store."

"It took you an hour to go to the liquor store?"

"Was I gone that long?"

"Yes."

"Huh. What's for dinner?"

"Whatever you're making."

Dan spun around. "Mom! What's for dinner?" Dan walked to the doorway. His mother was seated on the sofa.

"I bought some lunch meat," Peg replied.

"I don't want lunch meat, water, or paper towels for dinner."

"We could go out to dinner," Gene suggested.

"Can I talk to you for a second?" Richard asked.

"Hold on," Dan responded. "How about if I take you all out to dinner at Red's?"

"Red's?" Maxine asked. "Isn't there somewhere nicer we could go?"

"What's wrong with Red's?"

"It's a bar."

"And grill," Dan added.

"Red's is fine," said Gene.

"How much is that going to cost for all of us to go out to dinner?" asked Peg.

"It doesn't matter, Mom. You're not paying, I am."

"I bought stuff for sandwiches."

"We'll have that for lunch tomorrow."

"Maybe you guys should just go without me, and I'll stay here and have a sandwich."

"You're coming with us, Mom."

Peg got up off the couch. "Let me go see if I can do something with this hair," she said.

"Sonny, make me a drink. This could take a while."

"What the hell is that supposed to mean?" Peg shot back.

"What?" Gene asked.

"What the hell is—"

"I don't know what you're talking about, woman."

"Make you father that drink, Danny, then shove it up his ass."

"Ouch," said Gene. "Go fix your head."

Peg headed for the bathroom. "Prick," she whispered.

"What was that?" Gene called out.

"I don't know what you're talking about!" Peg hollered back.

"Dan, can we talk out back for a second?" Richard asked.

Dan craned his neck to see if Maxine was in the kitchen out of ear shot. "What is it?" he asked.

"The thumb drive."

"What about it?"

"Can we go outside and talk about it?"

Gene's eyes went from Richard to Dan and back. "Are you gonna tell me what's going on?"

"Can it wait till we get to Red's?" said Dan.

"I guess."

"Where is it?"

"The thumb drive?"

"Yeah."

"In my pocket."

"Don't lose it."

"How would I lose it?"

"Maybe I should hang onto it," Gene said.

"Rich will hang onto it," said Dan.

"What's going on, Sonny?"

"I'll fill you in later, Dad." Dan pulled out his cell and dialed.

"Danny Boy!" Joey Pantucco answered. "How those tiny little testicles hangin'?"

"Maggie is here," Dan said.

"Maggie who?"

"Maggie Harrison, the lawyer's daughter."

"Oh, yeah, her. I thought you wasn't supposed to talk to her."

"I'm not."

"Then why ya got 'er at your house?"

"She just showed up."

"That's bad, really bad."

"Yeah, I know, Joey. Have you heard anything?"

"Not a thing. Does Harrison know she's there?"

"He called me about an hour ago. He thinks she's here. He said if she wasn't home by tomorrow afternoon, that his guys were coming down to get her. What should I do?"

"For starters, have her home by tomorrow afternoon."

"She says Harrison is gonna kill her."

"Did you happen to ask her why he would want to kill her?"

"She mentioned something about money, but didn't elaborate."

"Elaborate?" Joey asked. "You get hit in the head with a dictionary, Coast? That's a pretty big word for you." Joey laughed.

"Stop kidding around, Joey."

"You gotta make her go home," Joey insisted.

"What if he kills her? That will be on me."

"What if you don't get her home and he kills you and Red, and who knows who else? That'll be on you too."

"Ugh! I don't know what to do."

"Just get her home, Coast." Joey ended the call.

"Dammit!" Dan said angrily, as quietly as he could.

"Any good news?" asked Richard.

"Yeah, Rich. It was all good news. I always say 'dammit!' when I get good news."

"You don't have to be a jerk."

"Yes, he does; he can't help it," said Gene. He rubbed his belly. "I'm hungry." He took a couple steps back and looked down the hallway. "Old woman! You ready?"

The bathroom light turned off; Peg walked out and down the hall. Her hair didn't look any different than it did when she entered the bathroom. "Did I hear someone say 'dammit'?" she asked.

"No," Dan answered. "Maxine, you ready to go?"

"Ready when you are," she hollered from the kitchen.

"Who's riding with who?" Gene asked.

"Rich and I will take my car," Dan replied, "and Maxine can ride with you and Mom in your rental."

"Sounds good," said Gene. "Let's move out."

Everyone exited the house and Maxine locked the door behind her. The group climbed into the two cars and were off.

Dan reached down and turned on his radio and tuned it to No Shoes Radio. Kenny Chesney was singing "Keys in the Conch Shell."

"Love this song," Dan said, and turned it up.

"Really?" Richard asked. He reached over and turned it down.

"Hey!"

"Don't you want to know what's on the thumb drive?"

"Of course I do. I just figured we would wait till we saw Red—oh, that reminds me." Dan pulled out his cell and phoned Skip.

"What's up, dude?"

"Hey, Skip. it's Dan, I need—"

"I can't come to the phone right—"

"Son of a bitch!" Dan waited for the beep. "Hey, Skip, it's Dan. Got a little problem. Meet us at Red's a soon as you can." He hung up.

"It's names and dates and times," said Richard.

"What?"

"The thumb drive. It's names, dates, and times. There's mention of deliveries, shipments. There's a whole folder on cops and judges who have been paid off, and what they've been paid off for."

"Shipments of what?" Dan asked.

"How would I know?"

"Does it mention the cops by name?'

"Name, badge number, address, and cell phone numbers. There's even a short bio about each guy."

"Wow, thorough."

"Yeah, almost too thorough," Richard agreed. "Why would a lawyer have this kind of information?"

"Seems odd to me, but then again, I've never been a drug dealer's attorney. My guidance counselor in high school never even mentioned drug dealer's attorney as a career."

"Why is everything a joke to you?"

"Ate a lot of lead paint chips when I was a kid."

"There's no off switch for you, is there?"

"Yes, but it's all the way down at the bottom of a tequila bottle."

"And you always have to get in the last word."

"Yut."

"It's annoying."

"My mother's dyin' words."

"I should have stayed in Texas."

"Hey, if you're ever down in Texas, look me up. Cha-cha-cha."

Richard slumped back in his seat. "What have I gotten myself into?"

Chapter Twenty-Six

Dan and Richard pulled into Red's parking lot with Gene driving in right behind them. Dan backed into his spot and Gene pulled into the spot next to him.

Gene swung open his door and climbed out. He stretched his arms over his head and took in a deep breath of island air. "We should really think about moving down here, Mother," he said.

"No you shouldn't," Dan answered. "You'd hate it down here."

"Yep," Gene continued, as everyone else exited the cars. "We could sell our place back home and buy a little place down here."

"Yeah, Dad, you could sell your place back home for two hundred grand, and then buy one here for two million. I'm sure you wouldn't have any problem making those mortgage payments."

"You're forgetting, Sonny, I got a wealthy son … and, I might be getting another wealthy son real soon." Gene glanced over the cars at Richard. He pointed and gave him a wink. "Ain't that right number two son?"

Richard winked and pointed back.

"He's older than me, Dad," said Dan. "So technically he's number one son. You know, just like in the old Charlie Chan movies."

"Holy Christ," said Richard. "I'm just going to let that one go."

"What?" Dan asked, shrugging his shoulders.

Richard closed the passenger side door and headed for the entrance. "Just shut up and come on, round eye."

"Hey! That's racist," said Dan.

"How can it be?" Richard asked with a grin. "I have a round-eyed brother."

"He's got ya there, Sonny," said Gene.

The group of five crossed the parking lot and went inside. Being a Monday, there were only about six other patrons in the bar. Two were seated at the bar, and the others were scattered about at tables. Ziggy Marley sang "Love Is My Religion" on the old Wurlitzer.

Gene's eyes went from the two surfboards suspended from the ceiling to The Endless Summer and Chasing Mavericks movie posters on the wall, to the Red Stripe and Islamorada Beer Company signs. "I love this place," he commented. "Maybe Red will give me a part-time bartending job to help out with that two million dollar mortgage."

"Yeah, maybe," Dan said.

"Bring it back to earth, Gene," said Peg. "We aren't moving anywhere."

"A boy can dream," said Gene.

"Yeah, a boy can," Peg responded, "but not an old fart like you."

Red looked up from the bar. "The Coasts!" he announced. Every head in the place turned to see what Red was talking about, and then turned back to their meals and drinks. "What brings you folks in on this fine evening?"

"I need one of Jocko's T-bone steaks in a bad way," Gene replied.

"Ooh, that sounds good," said Richard.

Red stepped back and pushed open the kitchen door a crack. "Abby!" he called out. "Come here and help me push a couple tables together."

"We got it, ya lazy bastard," said Dan.

"Never mind, Abby!" Red shouted.

Dan, Richard, and Gene pushed two four-tops together and placed six chairs around them. Gene took a seat at the head of the table with Peg to his right. Dan grabbed the chair at the other end with Maxine to his left, and Richard on his right. Red quickly left Cindy behind the bar, and joined his friends at their table.

"Haven't seen you guys since Christmas a couple years ago," Red stated. "What's new?"

"Not much," Peg replied.

"What's new with you?" Gene asked.

"Same old thing," said Red.

"Maxine tells me you have a new girlfriend," Peg said.

Red's face blushed a little. "Yeah."

"She said you had your first date on Friday night."

"Uh … yeah."

"How did it go?"

"Very good, Peg," Red said. "Thanks for asking." He glared at Dan when he said it.

"What?" Dan asked.

"You never asked me how my date went," Red tossed back.

"Oh," Dan chuckled. "I'm sorry. I would have asked, but I didn't care."

Gene and Richard laughed.

"He's a prick," said Richard.

"I don't know where he gets it," Gene said.

"Yeah," Peg said sarcastically. "I don't either."

"Red," Dan said, "did you still need Rich to look at that thing in your office?"

"What thing?" Red asked.

"That thing you were telling us about."

"Thing?"

"On your computer. *That thing.*"

"Oooh, *that* thing," Red said, finally catching on. "The thing in my office. The computer thing."

"Yeah, that thing."

"Yes, Dan, I do still need Richard to look at that thing."

Peg, Maxine, and Gene looked on in confusion.

"What thing?" Gene asked.

Red stood. "Can you look at that now, Rich?" he asked.

"Of course," Richard said. He got up from his chair.

Dan got up as well, and so did Gene.

"I want to see this *thing*," said Gene.

Maxine shook her head. "Morons," she whispered.

The four men crossed the floor and disappeared through the swinging kitchen door.

"Hey, Jocko," Gene said on his way by the grill. "Long time no see."

Jocko spun around and stuck out his hand. "Hey, Gene. How's it goin'?"

Gene winced a little when Jocko's giant hand squeezed his. Jocko slapped him on the shoulder with the other hand.

"What am I cookin' for ya tonight?" Jocko asked.

"I was hoping you had a nice thick T-bone somewhere in that cooler," Gene replied.

"Sure do."

Red opened his office door and stepped back as the other three entered. Red's office was small, just barely big enough for a desk, two chairs, a bookcase, and a computer stand. The men crowded in and Red shut the door.

Red looked from Dan to Richard. "I'm sorry, guys," he said, "but I can't for the life of me remember what I wanted you to look at in here."

Dan and Richard looked at each other and then back at Red.

"You didn't want us to look at anything," said Dan. "I was just trying to get you in here."

"So, there's no *thing*?" Gene asked.

"No, Dad."

"Huh. I had prepared myself for something really cool."

"Sorry to disappoint you," Dan responded. He turned to Richard. "Where's the thumb drive?"

"Right here in my pocket," Richard said. He reached into his front pocket and pulled it out.

Dan took it and handed it to Red. "Put this in your computer."

Red did as he was asked. "Now what?" he asked.

"Let's look at those files," Dan answered.

"Um," said Red.

"Click on that little blue circle in the bottom left hand corner," Richard instructed. "Now click on Computer." Richard waited a second. "Now click there, where it says Cruzer."

When Red did so a third window popped up with a list of files.

"What are we looking at?" Gene asked.

"They're files Maggie downloaded from her father's home office computer," Dan responded.

"Are you shittin' me?" Red asked.

"Let me in there," Richard said.

Red stepped back, and Richard sat down in the desk chair. Using his feet, he Fred Flintstoned it over to the computer stand, grabbed the mouse, and clicked on one of the files. "Here's a list of people," he said. "Below each name is an address and phone number. There's a brief description of each person and a little bio explaining who they are and how and when Harrison met them."

"Does it tell if they did anything illegal?" Dan asked.

"No," Richard said, "but here under this file"—he exited the current file and brought up another—"there's a list of people Harrison has represented in court."

"Representing people in court isn't illegal either," Gene pointed out.

"Is there anything on here we can use against him?" Dan asked.

Richard brought up a third file. "This one here is labeled COPS AND JUDGES WHO ARE FRIENDS."

"That sounds incriminating," Red said.

"Yeah," said Richard, "especially since there are payment amounts and dates the payments were made. Also a brief description of why the payments were made."

"We could threaten Harrison with this," said Dan. "We could tell him if he doesn't back off, and if anything happens to us or Maggie, we'll take this to the cops."

"If he kills us all," asked Richard, "then how do we get it to the police?"

"Well, in the movies," Red explained, "the good guys always give the evidence to a third party and—"

"It seems like I have to explain to you quite often that this isn't a movie," Dan interrupted.

"I know what he's saying, though," Gene said. "You give it to a third party with the instructions to turn it over to the authorities if anything happens to any of you."

"Why don't we just turn it over to the police *now*?" Richard asked.

"Maybe we should give it to the media," suggested Red.

"How many names are in that first file?" Dan asked.

Richard brought the file back up. "At least thirty names," he said.

Dan read through the names. "Oh crap," he said.

"What?" Red asked.

"I didn't notice before, but look at the tenth name down."

"Red counted down the list. "Joey Pantucco," he read aloud.

"Isn't that your friend in Miami?" Richard asked.

"He ain't really my friend," said Dan.

"He kinda is," Red said. He read on. "According to this, Harrison has known Joey since November 2009."

"Go back to that list of clients," Dan said. "See if Joey is on that list."

Richard clicked on the client list once again. Everyone read down the list to themselves. Joey was nowhere on that list.

"So, Harrison knows Joey, but Joey isn't a client," Dan surmised.

"What does that mean?" asked Gene.

"It probably just means that Joey has never been caught doing whatever it is he does," Richard answered. "So he's never needed Harrison's services."

Red turned to Dan. "What exactly does Joey do, anyway?" he asked.

Dan shrugged. "Mobster stuff," he replied.

"Can you narrow it down?" Richard asked.

"All I know is that he owns a few bars, restaurants, and strip clubs," said Dan. "He owns Sid's Beach Bar and Grill up in Islamorada."

"Hey," Gene asked, "is that the one with the giant flamingo on the billboard?"

"That's the one," Dan replied.

"All their steaks are flame-*ingo* broiled," Red added.

Richard looked back over his shoulder at Red. "What the hell is flame-*ingo* broiled?"

"I have no idea," Red replied. "But that's what the billboard said."

Dan's cell phone rang. "Hello?"

"Dan? It's Maggie."

"Everything all right?"

"Yes, but I'm starving and there's nothing to eat in this place."

"Did you check the cupboards?"

"Of course I checked the cupboards. There's two boxes of stale breakfast cereal, a can of chicken soup, and a few boxes of dry pasta."

"You don't like soup?"

"Seriously?"

"Okay, okay. I'll grab you something and bring it over."

"Thank you."

"It'll be about an hour or so."

"Why so long?"

"I have to eat my dinner first."

"What! Where are you? Are you at a restaurant?"

"Well, it's a bar and grill."

"You're something else," said Maggie disgustedly. "I'm sitting here starving to death, and you're out at a restaurant. Just get me something to eat as soon as possible, or I'll go get something myself."

"Don't you leave that hous—"

Maggie hung up.

"Dammit."

"What's the matter?" Gene asked.

"Maggie's hungry."

"Isn't there any food in that house?"

"Yes. She's just being over-dramatic. There's dry pasta *and* soup in the cupboard."

"Sounds like Thanksgiving dinner when I was a kid," said Red, shaking his head sadly.

"What are we gonna do next?" Richard asked.

"I'll just order her some take out," Dan replied.

"I mean about Harrison!"

"I don't know," Dan said. "I think better on a full stomach. Let's eat."

"Amen," said Gene.

"Yeah, I'm starving," Red agreed.

"Well then, by all means," Richard said, "let's go eat rather than figure out what to do about the guy who wants us all dead."

"My thoughts exactly," said Red.

Chapter Twenty-Seven

After dinner Maxine and Peg returned home in the Porsche and Dan, Gene, and Richard stayed behind at Red's for another drink. Dan and Gene both assured their wives that they wouldn't be out late. They both knew they were probably stretching the truth a little. Like father, like son.

It was another half hour before Skip finally showed up. When he arrived, the other four filled him in on the situation.

Dan ordered a burger and fries to go for Maggie. With the promise of a hefty tip, he even talked Cindy into delivering the food.

Skip, Dan, Red, and Richard all sat at the bar, with Red tending it. Everyone had a drink in front of them. Skip's drink was a ginger ale. He explained that he wasn't supposed to drink alcohol while on his medication.

"What do we do next?" Skip asked.

"I say we give Joey P a call and tell him we have Harrison's thumb drive, and that his name is on a list in a file on that thumb drive," Dan answered.

"What will that do?" Red asked.

"Let's just see if it makes him nervous. If he's nervous, that would mean everybody on that list might be nervous."

"And maybe we can convince them to get Harrison off our backs."

"Convince them?" Gene barked. "I think you mean *blackmail* them."

"Blackmailing them might convince them," Dan agreed.

"Yeah, it might convince them all that we should be dead," moaned Richard.

"That's a possibility," Dan said. He pulled out his cell phone and dialed.

"Danny Boy!" Joey Pantucco shouted into the phone. "You send Harrison's little girl home yet?"

"Not yet, Joey," Dan answered.

"Why?"

"I hid her."

"Hid her where?"

"I'd rather not say."

"Whatsamatta, Coast, you don't trust me?"

"I don't trust anybody right now, Joey. No offense."

"None taken."

"One more thing."

"What is it?"

"When Maggie showed up this afternoon, she had a thumb drive."

"A thumb drive?"

"Yeah. She had downloaded a bunch of files off her father's home office computer."

"Rambunctious little turd, ain't she?"

"Yeah. And there's one more thing."

"How many *one more things* are there, Coast?"

"Just one more *one more thing*."

"Let's hear it."

"You're name is on a list in one of those files."

There was a pause. Not a long pause, but long enough to tell Dan that Joey was contemplating his next words.

"What kind of list?" Joey asked.

"It's a list of names. Most of the names are Hispanic, Italian, and Russian." Dan covered the cell phone with the palm of his hand and looked to Richard. "Is that racist?" he whispered.

Richard shook his head. "You're an asshole."

"I never said I wasn't," whispered Dan.

Red and Skip chuckled quietly.

"Does it happen to mention why I'm on the list?" Joey asked.

"No, it just has your name, address, a phone number, and a little bit about you. It tells where and when Harrison first met you. There's mention of your businesses: strip clubs, restaurants, et cetera."

"Anything else on that thumb drive?"

"There's a file that contains names of cops and judges, and other city officials who have been paid off. It says who paid who, and for what. There's dates and meeting sites."

"Huh."

There was another pause, this one noticeably longer. "Why would Harrison have a file like this, Joey?" Dan asked, breaking the silence. "I realize many of the names in these files are his clients, but why would he be keeping a record of who they have paid off, and for what?"

"Well, Coast," Joey replied, "I'm gonna have to get back to you on this one. Where are you at?"

"We're at Red's."

"Stay put until you hear back from me. Is Maggie in a safe place?"

"Yes."

"Keep her there." Joey hung up.

"What did he say?" asked Red.

"He said to stay right here until I hear from him."

"Sounds like a good plan to me," Gene said. He slid his empty rocks glass across the bar. "Fill'er up, barkeep."

Dan pushed his glass to Red as well. "Me too," he said.

"We told Maxine and Peg we wouldn't be out that late," said Richard.

"'We told Maxine and Peg we wouldn't be out that late,'" Dan aped. "Don't be such a wuss, Rich."

"Yeah, Dick Bong," Skip joined in. "Don't be such a wuss."

"Wow," Richard said. He handed his empty glass to Red. "If you can't beat 'em, join 'em."

Red placed Gene's fresh drink in front of him.

"That's the spirit, Rich," said Gene, raising his glass into the air. "You'll be a Coast before you know it."

"Your liver will be the first to know it," said Red.

Chapter Twenty-Eight

The last four customers left Red's around ten o'clock that night, so Red decided to go ahead and lock the doors. Cindy had returned from her burger delivery to Maggie Harrison and was behind the bar with Red washing and drying bar glasses. Abby was busing the last two tables, and Jocko was shutting down the kitchen. It had been over three hours since Dan had spoken with Joey Pantucco.

Dan saw Richard look down at his wristwatch, which prompted Dan to look up at the clock over the bar.

"What do you think is taking Joey so long to call back?" Richard asked.

Dan shrugged. "Who knows," he replied. "Maybe he's doing some mobster shit."

"Should I make a pot of coffee?" Red asked.

"Good idea," Richard answered for the group.

Abby walked past the bar with a gray plastic tub filled with dishes, glasses, and silverware. Skip watched her as she walked by, and passed through the kitchen door.

"Who's the new girl?" Skip asked.

"Don't get any ideas," Dan said.

"I just asked her name," Skip said defensively.

"Her name's Abby," Red said. "She's Dan's contractor's girlfriend."

"And he hasn't painted my ceiling yet, so let's not piss him off by hitting on his girlfriend," Dan said.

"Let me know when he gets that ceiling painted," said Skip.

"Just you never mind."

Skip laughed. "I'm just yankin' your crank, Dan the Man."

Abby returned from the kitchen empty-handed.

"Everything all cleaned up in there?" Red asked. He scooped coffee out of a metal can and dumped it into the filter.

"All done," Abby said.

"You can take off if you want," Red told her.

"Abby looked at the clock. "Colton is picking me up," she said. "He should be here in a few minutes."

"Cup of coffee?"

"I'd rather have a bottle of beer."

Red stopped what he was doing and opened the cooler. "What can I get ya?"

"LandShark," she replied.

Red grabbed a bottle and twisted off the top. He started to set the bottle next to Skip, but then thought better of it. He sat it next to Gene.

Gene patted the seat of the bar stool next to him. "Jump right up here, kitten, I won't bite," he said.

"Don't believe him," Dan warned.

Abby smiled. "Just don't bite too hard."

The coffee maker quit dripping and Red asked who wanted a cup. Dan, Gene, Skip, Richard, and Cindy all took a cup. After pouring their mugs full of coffee he stared at the empty pot. "Why is it, a twelve cup coffee pot only fills five cups of coffee?" he griped.

"Why is it the window wash reservoir in your car only holds three and a half quarts of water?" Richard responded.

"How many licks *does* it take to get to the Tootsie Roll center of a Tootsie Pop?" asked Skip.

"The world may never know," Dan offered. "Someone play something on that jukebox. It's too quiet in here."

Even with the door shut the sound of tires rolling over the crushed stone parking lot could be heard inside.

"That must be Colton," said Abby. She took another swig of her drink and hopped off the stool. "I'm taking this beer with me. Goodnight, everybody. See y'all tomorrow."

Red walked around the bar and followed Abby to the door. "Let me get that door for ya," he said, "and I'll lock it behind you."

When he reached the door, Red spun the lock and pulled it open. There ya go. See ya tomor—"

Something whizzed past Red's face, and glasses on the shelf behind the bar shattered. He flinched, and so did everyone else in the room.

There was another whizzing sound and Abby's head snapped back.

Red watched as the young woman stumbled backwards. Her bottle of LandShark slipped from her finger tips and crashed to the floor. She toppled over backwards hit the wooden plank floor on her butt, and fell over onto her back. Her eyes were open and she stared up at the ceiling. A hole the size of a dime now decorated her forehead. A trail of blood ran from the hole, to her left eye, and dripped to the floor. Red stared down at the lifeless girl with confusion and horror.

"Shut that door!" Skip screamed. "Everybody get down!"

Red shoved the door closed and locked it. He dropped to his belly, and like a chubby anaconda, wiggled and crawled back toward the bar.

"Hit the lights!" Gene shouted.

"Where's the light switch?" Dan hollered.

Red looked toward the light switches behind the bar. He pointed. "There!"

Dan started in the direction of the switches, but Cindy was quicker. She reached up from her hiding spot behind the bar, and slapped the three switches into the off position. The room went dark, and the hum of the ceiling fan motors faded.

The kitchen door swung open. Jocko stood in the doorway, the light from the kitchen casting his long shadow on the bar room floor. "What the hell is going on in here?" he asked angrily.

The front plate glass window to the right of the entrance door shattered.

"Holy shit!" Jocko shouted. "What the—"

The sound of lead slicing through the air seemed eerily harsh in the silence of the dark bar and grill. More glasses shattered. Shards of glass hit the side of Jocko's face. He dove to the floor. The kitchen door swung shut behind him. Bullets smacked the wall five or six more times.

"Could you see who it was?" Dan asked in a loud whispering.

"I didn't see anyone," Red replied. He was still dragging himself along the floor.

"Are you hit?" Dan reached into his pocket for his cell phone. He dialed 911.

"I don't think so. But … Abby—"

"I know." Dan took the cell away from his ear and looked at the screen. "I'm not getting any service."

"Me neither," Cindy called out from behind the bar.

"Nothing here," Richard said.

"Whoever is out there is jamming the signal," said Skip.

"Isn't that against the law?" Red asked.

Dan glared at his friend. "Let's be sure to report them for that," he said. He threw his phone at Red. It bounced off the big guy's back and slid across the floor.

"Hey! What was that for?"

"Sorry, it slipped out of my hand."

"Sure it did."

"Where's the bar phone?" Skip asked.

"Behind the bar," Red answered.

No sooner did Red finish his sentence than the bar phone rang.

Cindy's hand reached up once again and lifted the receiver. She cautiously put the phone to her ear. "Red's

Bar and Grill," she announced. "How can I help you? Okay. Dan? It's for you."

"Is it Maxine?" Dan asked.

"No. It's the guy out front."

"Tell him I'm not here."

"What?"

"Just kidding. Hold on." Dan duck-walked behind the bar and took the phone from Cindy. "Hello?"

"Mr. Coast?" a voice asked.

"Speaking," Dan replied.

"Mr. Coast, Mr. Harrison has sent us to retrieve his daughter. Send her out, and everyone in there lives."

"Someone in here is already dead."

"That was just to let you know that we will kill everyone inside that building."

"What if I don't send her out?" Dan asked.

"Then everyone in there dies, of course."

"We have guns in here," Dan warned. "We could fight."

"In that case, the first two to die will be your girlfriend Maxine and your mother. Two of my men are inside your home as we speak."

"Son of a bitch," Dan whispered. "There's one problem."

"What would that be?"

"Maggie isn't here. I have her in a safe location."

"Give me the address, and one of my men will pick her up."

"I'll call you right back," Dan said, and hung up the phone.

"What do they want?" Richard asked.

"They want us to give up Maggie," Dan replied. "If we do, they'll let us live."

"I say we fight," Gene said sternly.

"He has two men at the house, Dad," said Dan. "He said they'll kill Maxine and Mom if we try anything."

"I say we *don't* fight then," Gene responded.

"How long do we have?" Skip asked.

"Until he calls back, I guess."

"That old pump action shotgun is in my office," said Red.

"Get it," Dan ordered.

Red was on his hands and knees and crawling as fast as he could toward the kitchen door.

"I've got a 9mm, a .38, and a sawed-off twelve gauge in my go bag," Skip said.

"Of course you do," Dan responded. "Where's your car parked?"

"On the side of the building, next to Red's pink Bug."

Richard cocked his head. "Pink Bug?"

"It's a long story," said Dan. He looked back at Skip. "You think you can get to your car?"

"If you fire Red's shotgun out that window, I can," Skip replied.

"Why the hell hasn't Joey called back yet?" Richard asked.

"We have to assume Joey is the one who told Harrison we were here," said Dan. "No one else knew we were here."

Red crawled back through the kitchen door and slid the shotgun across the floor to Dan. "There ya go, pal," he said.

"Shells?" Dan asked.

"Just the seven that are in there."

"Crap."

"What's the plan?" Jocko asked.

Every head turned toward the shattered front window when they heard the sound of another vehicle crossing the crushed stone parking lot.

"Shit," Dan said. "It's probably Colton." He jumped up and ran, stooping, over to the window. He watched as Colton's truck came to a stop right in front. For the first time Dan could see the shooter's vehicle on the other side of the parking lot, two spaces over from Gene's rental. It was a black Lincoln Navigator; there was no sign of the shooters.

Colton shut off his engine and opened his door.

"Get back in your truck!" Dan shouted.

Colton stopped and looked around.

"Get back in your truck!" Dan shouted again.

Colton squinted to see through the window into the darkness. "What?" he asked. He started walking toward the front door and made it up two steps before a single pop rang out. Colton arched his back and tumbled forward. He was dead before he hit the porch floor.

"God dammit!" Dan screamed. Two more bullets hit the front door and shattered some of the remaining glass in the window. Dan ducked back behind the wall. Another shot cut through the air.

Richard let out a gasp, and a loud moan. "I'm hit," he cried out. "Jesus Christ, I'm hit! Dan!"

Gene, Skip, and Dan all moved toward Richard as quickly as they could. Skip got to him first.

"Where are you hit?" Skip asked.

"My shoulder!"

Skip pulled off his T-shirt and pressed it against the wound. "Gene, keep pressure on this."

Gene complied. "It's gonna be okay, Rich," he said.

The bar phone rang again.

Dan crawled around the bar on his knees and one hand. He carried the shotgun in the other.

"What happened out there?" Red asked.

"They shot Colton."

"Son of a bitch."

Dan got behind the bar and reached up and grabbed the phone. "You didn't have to kill him, you piece of shit!" he hollered into the phone.

"That's all on you," said the caller. "The longer we stay here, more people will die."

"I'll take you to Maggie," Dan said defeatedly.

"Not you," said the caller. "Someone else."

Dan dropped his head and stared into the floor. "Fine," he said. "Someone will be right out."

"Don't try anything stupid."

Dan hung up the phone.

"What did they say?" Red asked.

"Someone has to go with one of his guys to get Maggie. He said it couldn't be me."

"I'll go," said Jocko.

"Are you sure?" Dan asked.

"Yeah."

"Okay, listen," Dan said. "Whatever happens, Jocko, that guy who goes with you, he can't make it to Maxine's house alive."

Jocko nodded his head. "Understood," he said. He stood up and started for the door.

"Wait," Skip said.

Everyone looked over at him

"As soon as Jocko walks out that front door, Dan, I'll go out the bathroom window, and run to your house. I'll—"

"Run to my house?" Dan interrupted. ""What the hell—"

"Running full speed, I can be there in five minutes, Dan," Skip assured him. "I'll take out the men at your house."

"With what?" Dan asked. "You don't have a weapon."

"There's a bunch of butcher knives in that kitchen," said Skip. He reached into his pocket and pulled out his car keys. He tossed them to Red. "Give me fifteen minutes, then start shooting at those assholes. Red, while Dan's covering you, you get to my Thing and get the go bag out of the trunk. There's three weapons in that bag. Use them."

"Cindy!" Dan called out, "get out here and keep pressure on Rich's wound. I'm gonna need my dad to fire one of those weapons when we get them."

Skip looked up at Jocko. "Go ahead," he said.

Gene slid his car keys across the bar floor. "Take my car, Jocko," he said. "The gray Camry."

Jocko went out the front door, and Skip hurried to the kitchen. He came back into the bar carrying a butcher knife and a smaller steak knife.

Skip twirled both knives in his hands, flipped them into the air, and caught them both by the handles. He made quick stabbing motions like he was in a knife fight. "These should do the trick," he said

"Show-off," said Dan.

Skip grinned. "I'll be back as quick as I can, guys." he turned and ran to the men's room.

Dan hurried back to the window and peeked around the wall. He watched as Jocko crossed the parking lot, his hands in the air. One of the unknown gunmen frisked him. Jocko climbed into the driver's seat of Gene's car. The man who frisked him climbed into the passenger seat. A second goon climbed into the backseat.

Shit, Dan thought. He had hoped only one man would be going with Jocko.

The car started, and Jocko drove out of the parking lot.

"Good luck," Dan whispered.

Chapter Twenty-Nine

Jocko drove Gene's rented Camry down White Street and hung a right onto Flagler Avenue. He glanced into the rear view mirror. The guy in the back seat blocked most of the rear window.

"Can you slide over a bit, pal?" Jocko asked. "I can't see behind me." He reached up and adjusted the mirror.

The guy in the back locked eyes with Jocko. He didn't say a word.

Jocko looked over at Goon One, in the front passenger seat. "Your friend's not very talkative," he said.

"Shut the fuck up," said the thug.

"Yeah," said Goon Two, "shut the fuck up."

Jocko heard Goon Two disengage the slide lock on his pistol and pull back the slide. Several scenarios went through Jocko's head all at once. He imagined himself slamming his fist into Goon One's throat. Then he imagined Goon Two shooting him in the back of the head; that was not how Jocko wanted the night to end.

I could swerve into an oncoming car, Jocko thought. *But that could kill an innocent person. I could slam on the brakes. Goon Two isn't wearing his seat belt. If I'm lucky, he would fly forward, I could wrestle the gun out of his hand, and shoot both of them. What are the odds that would work?*

As they passed Leon Street, Goon One's cell phone rang. "Yeah," he answered. "How much farther?" he asked Jocko.

"It's right up here," Jocko lied. "About two minutes."

"Roger that," said Goon One. He hung up.

"Fuck it," Jocko whispered to himself. He punched the gas petal to the floorboard.

"What the hell are you doing?" shouted Goon Two.

"Slow down!" said Goon One. Out of the corner of his eye Jocko saw him release his seat belt and reach for his weapon, holstered under his arm.

Jocko felt Goon Two's cold steel barrel press against the back of his neck. He yanked the wheel hard left, crossing the westbound lane.

Jocko glanced down at the speedometer—72MPH. The vehicle jumped the curb, barreled across the parking lot, and smashed into the front of Advance Auto Parts. There was no explosion, like in the movies. There was only one loud crash, followed by the continuous wailing of the car horn. Steam rose up from the mangled radiator and curled around and over the store's canopy.

Chapter Thirty

Skip was running shirtless down Atlantic Boulevard as fast as he could, a knife in each hand. He thought back to how many times his mother had told him not to run with scissors.

He turned the corner onto Grove Street and then cut across someone's lawn onto Sky View Street. When he was halfway down the street he turned and ran through a vacant lot, and ended up behind Edna McGee's house. Skip slowed to a jog and scanned Beach View Street. He moved to a position at the corner of Edna's house and stopped. His heart continued to pound.

Dan's living room light was on and the curtains were open. A black Lincoln Navigator, just like the one at Red's, sat parked in the street in front of Dan's house. Skip could see one head in the vehicle. He crouched down and made his way to the Navigator for a better look. He peeked through the rear passenger side window. A man in a black T-shirt sat behind the steering wheel. His arm hung out the open window, a lit cigarette between two fingers. The radio was on and music played quietly.

Skip duck-walked around the back of the vehicle and up the side. When he was right below the driver's side window he grabbed the man's arm with his left hand, and quickly rose up, putting the blade of the butcher knife against the man's throat.

The guy tried to pull back, but the headrest prevented him from doing so.

"How many of you are there?" Skip asked quietly.

The guy didn't answer.

Skip pushed the knife harder into the man's throat. "How many?"

"Two of us."

"Where's your partner?"

"He's inside the house."

"Slowly remove your weapon and drop it outside," Skip calmly ordered.

The man obeyed, dropping his 9mm on the pavement at Skip's feet.

"Thanks, dude," Skip said. He pulled the knife away from the man's head, turned it slightly, and smashed the butt of the handle into the bridge of the guy's nose. Blood instantly ran down the man's lip like the flood gates had just been opened.

"Agh!" the guy hollered. His hands went to his face.

"Here, hold this," Skip said, handing the man the butcher knife.

The guy took the knife, and in one swift motion Skip placed one hand on the back of the man's head and with his other hand on the guy's jaw, effortlessly snapped his neck. The man's lifeless body slumped forward.

Skip pushed him over in the seat, and then turned toward the house. He bent down and picked up the weapon. As he walked toward Dan's house, he ejected the magazine and checked the ammo. He jammed the magazine back into the grip and yanked back the slide.

"What's going on out there?" Edna McGee hollered from her front porch. "Who's out there?"

"Hey, Mrs. McGee," Skip hollered back without diverting his attention away from Dan's house. "It's just me, Skip."

"Oh, okay, sweetie," said Edna. "Nice night."

"Yes it is." As he walked up the steps he could see the other black T-shirted thug standing in Dan's living room, his arms folded across his chest. Maxine and Peg sat on the couch.

Skip crossed the porch, kicked open the front door, and put nine rounds into the man's chest before he had time to react.

Peg and Maxine both screamed.

"Is anyone else here?" Skip asked.

"There's a man out front," Maxine replied.

"He's already dead," said Skip. "Where's Dan's weapon?"

"In the nightstand."

"Danny has a weapon?" Peg asked. "Why does Danny have a weapon?"

"Get it," Skip ordered.

Maxine stood. "Where's Dan?" she asked.

"He's at Red's. He's fine. Get his gun."

Maxine ran to the bedroom and returned seconds later with Dan's chrome 9mm. She handed it to Skip.

"Where're the keys to the Porsche?"

Maxine turned and grabbed them off the small round table that holds Alex's photograph. "Here."

Skip took the keys. "Call the police. I have to go." He turned and ran back out the busted door.

Chapter Thirty-One

"Well, that makes fifteen minutes," said Gene.

Red slowly got to his feet.

"You ready?" Dan asked.

"I'm ready," Red responded.

"Wait."

What?"

"I'll go," said Dan. "Give me the keys to the Thing."

"Don't be stupid," Red said. "I'm going. Just cover me."

Dan nodded. "Are you sure?"

"Oh my God," Richard groaned. "If you guys are gonna kiss, then kiss, but one of you has to go now. I'm bleeding to death here."

Red started for the back door. Dan waited.

Red yanked open the door and Dan started firing. As he fired the pump action shotgun he watched the three men he could see near the Navigator scatter.

Red ran out the back door, then ran back inside seconds later, empty-handed. He swung the door shut behind him, and hit the floor on his belly.

Dan emptied his weapon and jumped back behind the wall. "Where's the go bag?" he shouted.

"I didn't make it that far!" Red hollered back.

"Why not?"

"Someone started shooting at me."

"You have any more shells for this thing?"

"Of course."

"Get them."

"They're at my house."

Dan shook his head.

"What now?" asked Gene.

The three men out front opened fire. The silencers on their weapons made it seem as the destruction inside the bar was taking place by magic. Everyone inside lay down and covered their heads as bullets shattered glasses, windows, and booze bottles. Wood splinters flew about the room. One of the suspended surfboards hit the floor next to Dan. A ceiling fan blade disconnected from the motor and sailed across the room, smashing the glass front of the Wurlitzer.

"Dammit!" Red shouted.

All at once the shooting stopped. Everyone remained still.

Skip emerged from the bathroom holding the two pistols. Dan looked up. Skip tossed him his 9mm.

"Maxine and my mom?" Dan asked.

"They're both fine," Skip replied.

Their heads turned toward the parking lot when they heard the vehicle doors slamming. The engine started.

Skip ran out the front door, with Dan close behind him. The two men ran to the center of the parking lot as the Navigator was speeding away. Both men raised their weapons and began firing. The rear window of the Navigator exploded.

Dan and Skip continued to pull their triggers until their weapons were empty. They watched as the black Lincoln turned the corner and disappeared from sight.

"Well, that was fun," Dan said.

"You know it, bro," Skip responded.

The two men turned and hurried back to the bar.

Skip knelt down next to Colton and checked for a pulse. "He's dead."

"Yeah," Dan said, "I figured."

When they got back inside, Gene was already dialing 911. Judging by the sounds of sirens in the distance, it probably wasn't necessary.

Red grabbed a table cloth off one of the tables and spread it over Abby's body. Dan saw what Red was doing and yanked another table cloth off the table nearest him. He turned and went back through the front door.

As Dan spread the cloth over Colton's body his cell phone rang. "Yeah, Joey?" he answered.

"Hey, Coast," said Joey. "You okay?"

"I'm just fine. How are you?"

"Is it over?"

"It's over."

"They left?"

"Yes. But, why?"

"It took me awhile, but I got a hold of their boss and had him call them off."

"Their boss?" Dan asked. "You mean, Harrison?"

"No, not Harrison. Those men didn't work for Harrison. They were just assigned by one of his clients to protect him."

"Isn't Harrison gonna be pissed when he finds out what you did?"

"No," Joey replied. "Harrison is probably already dead."

"Oh," said Dan. "Good."

Dan paused for a second. "Ya know, Joey, for a minute there, I thought it was you who sicced those goons on us."

Joey chuckled. "Don't be ridiculous, Coast. I love you guys. I'll call you back tomorrow."

"What time—"

Joey hung up.

Red picked up the bar phone and dialed. He waited, but there was no answer. "Come on, Jocko, pick up."

Jocko's phone went to voice mail.

Red hung up and dialed again. There was still no answer. "Dammit!" he said.

Sirens could be heard off in the distance.

"I'm sure Jocko will be walking back through the door in no time at all," said Dan.

Red hung up the phone. "Yeah, probably." He flipped the lights back on. Only one bulb lit, the others had all been shot out during the last volley of shots.

"Holy shit, Red Man," said Skip. "This place is a mess."

Red stood behind the bar, his eyes going from one broken beer sign to the other. His movie posters and even his autographed photo of Ernest Hemingway were riddled with bullet holes.

"Anyone need a drink?" Red asked, as he poured one for himself. "I think I have about five glasses left."

Chapter Thirty-Two

"Ashes to ashes, dust to dust," the reverend said, as he stood at the head of Jocko's grave, two days later.

Maxine, Peg, Cindy, and Lydia Bell, Jocko's only sibling, sat in metal folding chairs at the graveside. Dan, Red, Skip, Richard, Gene, and about thirty other folks stood behind the chairs, and near the foot of the grave. Dan and Red were looking uncomfortable in their suits. And even Skip wore a tie and dress shirt with his board shorts and Vans. Richard stood next to Gene, his arm in a sling.

As the reverend spoke, Dan looked around the crowd. "Looks like Jocko had a lot of friends," he whispered.

"Looks that way," Red whispered back.

Dan reached forward and put his hand on Maxine's shoulder. She reached up and put her hand on his, and gave a slight squeeze. He looked up at the sky and watched the gray clouds float by for a second, wondering if the rain would at least hold off until after the burial. It was hard to imagine a world without Jocko sticking his head through the kitchen door and saying, "Hey, Coast," and then busting Dan's balls for being pussy-whipped.

Out of respect for the deceased, Rick Carver had delayed his investigation into Dan and his cohorts once again taking the law into their own hands. The mitigating circumstances would likely clear them of any wrong doing. Rick took Jocko's death hard, and while he couldn't attend the funeral, he sent a lovely wreath on behalf of himself and the police department. He shared the general opinion that Jocko was a brave man who died a hero's death.

Meanwhile, Rick's forensic team had pieced together what went down the night Jobe "Jocko" Morris died. The passenger side air bag was turned off, and didn't deploy. Goon One—who wasn't wearing his seatbelt—hit the dashboard, killing him instantly. Goon Two, also unrestrained, went through the windshield and hit the block wall of Advance Auto Parts. The coroner said almost every bone in his body was fractured. Jocko's air bag opened. The coroner said the only mark on Jocko's body was where Goon Two's bullet, after ripping through the front seat, entered his back and pierced his aorta.

"Thank you for coming," said the reverend. "After the burial, Jocko's friends and family have invited everyone back to Red's Bar and Grill—where Jocko has worked for the past twenty-five years—for food and drinks."

"Twenty-five years?" Dan asked.

"Yeah," Red replied. "He was there way before me."

As the crowd dispersed, Dan and Red stayed by the grave, staring into the hole.

"This really sucks," Red said.

"It sure does," Dan agreed. "At least he took those two bastards out with him."

"Have you heard anything about Colton and Abby's funerals?"

"Colton's funeral is Friday, and Abby's parents are having her body flown back to Georgia to be buried."

"You going to Colton's funeral?"

"I guess I should." Dan replied. "Maybe some of his contractor buddies will be there. I still need my ceiling painted."

"Wow, you're a prick." Red turned and walked toward the street.

"I never said I wasn't."

*****

Cindy and Red had pulled several tables together to accommodate the large groups of mourners. Dan, his parents, Maxine, Bev, Richard, and Skip all sat at one of the tables. Empty beer bottles and glasses were scattered about the table top.

After the crowd thinned, Red, Cindy, and her boyfriend, Derek, joined the group.

"It's too quiet in here," Dan said. "Put a couple bucks in that jukeb—oh, crap, that's right." He glanced over his shoulder at the pathetic looking Wurlitzer. "I think this will be the third time since I've known you that you had to have that thing repaired."

"Yeah," Red responded, "I should just throw the damn thing out and get one of those digital ones. They play any song you can think of."

"I only want to think about the songs that are already in that one," said Dan. "If I had to choose from thousands of songs, I would never be able to make up my mind."

"True dat, Dan the Man," said Skip. "I don't need that kind of stress in my life."

Red scanned the room. "Look at this place," he said. "What a friggin' mess."

"It could have been a lot worse," Gene offered.

"Yes, it could have," Peg agreed, placing her hand on top of Gene's. "Crazy old fool," she said.

"Hey, I resemble that," Gene said, laughing. "Just think of the great story we have to tell at the Moose Club Wednesday night, old woman."

"Wednesday night?" Skip asked.

"Meatloaf night," Dan explained.

"Ah."

"We're just lucky Harrison's men left when they did," Richard said.

"We're lucky Joey P got a hold of the people Harrison worked for and told them about the thumb drive," said Dan. "Evidently, Harrison and his wife had been collecting data on every bit of wrong doing his clients were involved in."

"I can't believe Harrison thought he could blackmail those people," said Red, shaking his head. "What an idiot."

"According to Joey," Dan continued, "Harrison did finally come to his senses and decide against blackmailing them, but his wife wanted out and threatened to go to the cops. That's when Harrison decided to have her killed and blamed it on Maggie's boyfriend."

"That explains why he wanted his wife out of the picture," said Richard. "But why did he want Maggie dead?"

Dan shrugged. "Who knows? Maybe she was asking too many questions after her mother's death. I guess we'll never know for sure."

"No sign of Harrison?" Skip asked.

"Nope," Dan replied. "Joey said he disappeared an hour or so after his phone call."

"You think he escaped?" asked Richard.

"I think he's sleeping with the fishes," said Dan.

"Wow, I never heard anyone say that before, and mean it," Richard said.

"So, even though Harrison decided not to blackmail his clients, they still killed him," Red said.

"They probably didn't think they could trust him anymore," said Dan.

"But they trust us?" Richard asked.

"I guess Joey put in a really good word for us."

"Where's the thumb drive now?" Skip asked.

"I'm keeping it in a safe place until I hand deliver it to Joey Friday morning."

"Where is the safe place?" Red asked.

"Between my butt cheeks," Dan replied.

"Are you serious?"

"No, I'm not serious, ya moron," Dan shot back. "It's in the drawer in my nightstand."

The group chuckled and Dan lifted his tequila, Seven, and lime into the air. "To Jocko," he said. "God's eatin' a damn good T-bone steak tonight."

Everyone raised their glasses. "To Jocko!"

Chapter Thirty-Three

Friday afternoon, on his way back from delivering the thumb drive to Joey Pantucco, Dan got a call from Doc Briddle's office. The DNA results were in. He stopped by the office and picked up the envelope and drove straight home.

When Dan pulled his Porsche into the driveway, he could see his father and Richard sitting in the Adirondack chairs next to the fire pit. Dan climbed out of the car and carried the envelope down the driveway and into the back yard. Buddy lay on the ground next to Richard's chair.

"Dad, where's Mom?" Dan called out.

"I killed her," said Gene.

"Dad."

"She's in the house."

"Mom!" Dan hollered. "Maxine!" He walked over and grabbed the folding lawn chair, unfolded it, and sat down. He held the envelope to his forehead like Carnac the

Magnificent. "I have in this envelope the results from the DNA test."

Gene and Richard sat forward in their chairs.

"Maxine!" Dan yelled. "We should get Mom and Maxine out here too."

"What?" Maxine shouted.

"I've got the DNA results!"

Maxine and Peg hurried out of the house and trotted down the gravel path to the fire pit.

"What does it say?" Peg asked.

"I haven't opened it yet," Dan said. "Is everyone ready?"

"Ready," everyone said.

Dan took a deep breath and started to open the envelope.

All heads turned toward the road when they heard Skip's Volkswagen Thing pull up out front and sputter to a stop.

"What the Christ?" Dan whispered.

A few seconds later, Skip and Red bumbled down the path to the backyard.

"What's up, Coasts?" Red asked.

"We got the DNA results back," Gene answered.

"What's the verdict?" Skip asked.

"Haven't opened them yet," Richard answered.

"Okay," said Dan. "Is everybody ready?"

"Ready," everyone responded.

Dan tore at the corner of the envelope.

"Yoo-hoo!" Edna McGee called out. She was carrying a plate of cookies.

"Are you shittin' me?" Dan grumbled quietly.

"Richard!" Edna sang out. "I made you those peanut butter cookies like I promised."

Richard stood. "Gee, thanks, Edna," he said. "We just got the DNA results back. Dan's about to read them."

"Oh, my goodness," Edna crowed. "Maxine told me you were getting one done. This is so exciting."

Richard offered his chair to Edna and she sat down. He placed the plate of cookies on the picnic table.

All eyes were on Dan. "Ready?"

Can I get a cookie first?" Red asked.

"Yeah, me too," said Skip.

"No," Dan replied. "Ready."

Dan tore open the envelope and pulled out the paper inside. Before unfolding it, he paused and looked at Gene. Dad, he said, "If we find out today that Rich *is* your son, that means you've spent the last forty-something years being a dead beat dad. Are you willing to step up and take responsibility for Richard?"

"You don't know me," Gene shot back. "I take care of my kids."

"It's time to kick that dog to the curb!" Skip shouted.

"You need to dump that zero and get yourself a hero!" Red shouted, and began pumping his fist in the air. "Maury! Maury! Maur—"

"Shut up, you morons!" Maxine hollered.

Dan unfolded the paper. "Dad," he said.

"Yes?" Gene responded.

"You *are* my father."

Gene glanced over at Peg. "And all this time I thought it was the milkman," he quipped.

"Shut up, you old fool," Peg said. "What about Richard?"

"Dad."

"Yes?"

All eyes were focused on Dan.

"Drum roll please," said Dan.

Skip began performing his best drum roll imitation, complete with hand gestures and vibrating his tongue against the roof of his mouth.

"Gene Coast," Dan continued, "Richard Bong … *is* your son."

"I knew it!" Peg shouted. She was the first one to reach Richard with a great big welcome to the family hug.

As Richard was having the life squeezed out of him, he turned and looked in Dan's direction. He smiled and nodded his head. Dan returned the gesture with another nod.

Skip wiped the tears from his eyes as he made his way to Richard. He stuck out his hand, and they shook. "Welcome to the family, Dick Bong," he said.

"Thanks, Skip Stoner," Richard replied.

Gene was next with the hugs, and Dan waited to take his turn last. He and Richard shook hands and Dan said, "We got a lot of catching up to do."

"You got that right, brother," Richard replied. "But let's do some of that catching up in Texas. Florida is just too damn dangerous."

Dan chuckled and pulled his new brother in for a hug.

"Wow," Maxine said. "A hug. He doesn't do that very often."

"Specially with other guys," Red added.

"Jealous?" Dan asked. He turned and pulled Red into a hug as well.

"Two hugs in one day," said Peg. "A new record."

"Take advantage of it," Dan said. "Anybody else? It's now or never."

Gene went in for his hug, and so did Skip.

Peg turned and threw her arms around Maxine. "I need one too. Come on, Edna. Get in here."

"This is just like the end of a Nicholas Sparks movie," Skip sobbed, the tears streaming down his face. "I'm gonna be even worse at you guys' wedding. Did you set a date yet?"

"Shut up," said Dan.

The End

Coming Soon:

Fernandina Beach Mysteries
Serial Maintenance

Sunrise City 4
Dig Two Grave

ALSO BY RODNEY RIESEL

From the Tales of Dan Coast Series

Sleeping Dogs Lie
Ocean Floors
The Coast of Christmas Past
Ship of Fools
Double Trouble
Most Likely to Die
Deadly Moves
On the Wagon
No Enemies Here
Neighborhood Watch

Jake Stellar Series

North Murder Beach
Beach Shoot
When Death Returns
The Obedience of Fools
Dead in the Water
Excited About Nothing

The Dunquin Cove Series

The Man in Room Number Four
Return to Dunquin Cove
Local Hero

Sunrise City Series
Sunrise City
Sunrise City 2: From Bad to Worse
Sunrise City 3: Never Strikes Twice

Fernandina Beach Mysteries

Maintenance Required
High Maintenance

From Here to There: A Collection of Short Stories